THE KING OF THE COPPER MOUNTAINS

PAUL BIEGEL

ENGLISH VERSION BY
GILLIAN HUME AND PAUL BIEGEL

ILLUSTRATED BY SALLY J COLLINS

WWW.STRIDENTPUBLISHING.CO.UK

Published by
Strident Publishing Ltd

22 Strathwhillan Drive
The Orchard, Hairmyres
East Kilbride G75 8GT

Tel: +44 (0) 1355 220588
info@stridentpublishing.co.uk
www.stridentpublishing.co.uk

A catalogue record for this book is
available from the British Library.

ISBN 978-1-905537-14-3

English translation © J M Dent & Sons Ltd and Franklin Watts, Inc 1969
Illustrations © Sally J Collins 2007

First published in Holland under the title HET SLEUTELKRUID C
by Uitgeversmaatschappij Holland – Haarlem 1965

Originally published in the UK by J M Dent & Sons Ltd,
now part of the Orion Publishing Group Ltd

This edition by Strident Publishing Limited, 2009

Typeset in Optima
Designed by Sallie Moffat

CHAPTER ONE

If you travel far to the south you will come to the blue sea. It has not always been so; in earlier times the copper mountains stood there instead, so dazzling in the sunshine that you could not look at them.

At the foot of the mountains there was an avenue leading to the door of a castle full of copper corridors and rooms, and in the castle lived the old king, Mansolain.

King Mansolain had a beard that spread about his feet like a rug, and on it slept a hare, the only creature that still cared for him now that King Mansolain was almost forgotten.

For more than a thousand years already he had reigned over all the animals and dwarfs, and over the dragons too while they were still in existence. But as nowadays he never went out, there was scarcely anyone left who knew him. His servants had died one after the other until only the hare remained. So these two lived quietly together in the copper castle until the king began to cough so badly that his beard shook and the hare grew very anxious.

The Wonder Doctor was sent for to examine the king. When he had finished he took the hare into another room and said: 'I put my ear to His Majesty's chest and through his beard I heard a peeping and a whistling. His heart ticks unevenly like a crooked clock that is running down, and that is the result of old age.'

The hare looked worried.

'Within a week the king will be dead,' said the Wonder Doctor.

The hare started to sob.

'His heart needs a speeder-up that would work like the key of a clock,' said the Wonder Doctor, 'so that it will tick faster and normally again.'

The hare looked up. 'Is there such a remedy?' he asked.

'Yes, there is,' said the Wonder Doctor. 'A potion made from the Golden Speedwell. But I would have to travel many miles to find this rare plant, so that when I got back it might be too late.'

The hare's ears drooped. 'Is there no other medicine that we could use in the meantime?' he asked.

'Not one you swallow,' said the Wonder Doctor, 'but maybe something else.' He took off his learned-looking spectacles and went on: 'The king's heart should beat soundly and evenly once a day, then he might pull through. So, each evening before he retires, you must tell him a story full of excitement.'

The hare had pricked up his ears now but they drooped again. 'I told my last story seven years ago,' he said. 'And as for books, the king knows them all by heart.'

The Wonder Doctor thought for a long time. Then he put on his learned-looking spectacles again, took his hat and his little black bag and said: 'I'm going to fetch some leaves of the Golden Speedwell. On my way I'll tell everybody I meet that whoever knows a story should go to the castle in the copper mountains and tell it to the king. I only hope there will be enough stories for all the days I'll be away, but that I'll know when I get back with the Golden Speedwell. God save the king. Good day!' And the Wonder Doctor disappeared through the door, shutting it with a bang that echoed through the copper corridors.

For a long time the hare stood deep in thought. Then he went off to the kitchen to make up the fire ready for the roast meat and pudding that the king liked so much.

Late that evening the king was coughing worse than ever and was just going to bed when there was a thundering knock on the door. The hare took the lantern from the hook, lit the candle inside it, and went to the front door.

'Who's there?' he cried.

'A storyteller!' replied the hoarse voice.

The hare swung open the door and held the lantern high above his head to see who this storyteller might be.

The flickering candlelight fell on a fierce-looking wolf who at once held a paw in front of his green eyes. 'Not so much light, if you please,' he grumbled, 'and let me in quickly.' He pushed the hare aside and dragged the door shut behind him. 'All right mister! Now you'd better take me to the king. I have a story that will buck him up.'

'Did the Wonder Doctor send you?' the hare asked.

'What do you think!' snapped the wolf.

As they walked through the corridors the hare thought to himself how dangerous it was to let such a complete stranger into the castle. Who knows what wicked deeds this wolf may have done in the past?

'What does this mean?' the king asked when he saw the wolf.

'Sire, a visitor,' the hare said solemnly.

'Really?' said the king. He shifted in his chair and polished his spectacles with his beard. 'It's a long time, about sixty years I should think, since anyone came to see me.'

To the hare's astonishment this fierce-looking wolf bowed low to the king and said; 'Great thousand-year-old king of us all, I bow to you – though to nobody else. Hearing that you were ill, I came to tell you a story, a thrilling adventure that has never been told before.'

'Really?' said the king again, peering at the wolf with dim eyes. 'I believe I knew your grandfather,' he said. 'Wasn't he the wolf Esmaril...or was he Jago?'

'My grandfather was the terrible Woe-Wolf of the Bare Flank,' the wolf said. 'And my story is about him. Listen...'

THE WOLF'S STORY

Long ago, away up in the dark pinewoods of the north, there was a clearing which nobody ever dared enter. The trees stood in a circle round a great heap of stones, jagged like a witch's teeth. And indeed a witch lived in that very spot, or so thought all the wolves. Only the Woe-Wolf thought otherwise.'

'There are no such things as witches!' he said. 'And one day, if I ever have time, I'll go to that place and howl at the top of my voice and then you'll see for yourself she won't appear!'

While he was speaking, the wolves beside him thought that they heard the sound of distant laughter, though that, of course, might have been imagination.

The Woe-Wolf glared at them with fierce eyes. 'Don't just stand there trembling!' he cried. 'Come on, let's hunt for something good to eat!'

So off they went, following him two by two until they came to open country where they could run ten abreast.

A little later, when the sun went down and dusk began to fall, they met a huge buffalo that had strayed from the herd. This creature was nearly three times the size of the Woe-Wolf, but without a moment's hesitation and as though his legs were steel springs, he leapt onto its neck.

Then followed a terrible fight in which the Woe-Wolf was jerked to and fro so violently that heaven and earth seemed to him to mix together like porridge.

But he never let go for an instant and in the end the buffalo fell dead.

It was a great victory and would certainly have led to quite a celebration had a strange thing not occurred. Suddenly there was a savage snorting behind them and when the Woe-Wolf looked round he saw a still bigger, white buffalo. It immediately wheeled about and set off in the direction of the forest.

'*Woe, woe*, wolves!' cried the Woe-Wolf. 'After him! He's the one for us!'

He at once started after the pale form that galloped through the darkness. Soon, he was among the trees, but though their trunks bruised his bones and the brambles tore his coat, he never lost sight of his prey.

'*Woe, woe!*' he cried again, but the ghostly white of the buffalo became fainter and fainter and finally disappeared.

The wolf came to a halt and pricked up his ears. There was no longer any sound of trampling hoofs, no snorting, no cracking of branches. Was the buffalo hiding?

Stealthily the wolf crept forward, nose to the ground, and so came to the clearing where the dark pines stood in a circle round the heap of weird stones.

'Aha, that's where he'll be!' the Woe-Wolf thought and quickly leapt on top of the heap. But the stones parted, or so it seemed to him, and no buffalo was to be seen, nothing but more stones, which now completely surrounded him.

'*Woe, woe!*' the wolf howled.

'*Woe-oe-oe-oe!*', sounded from seven sides as though seven wolves were answering.

'I'm here!' he cried, thinking the wolves had followed him.

But from seven sides came the answer: '*Here-ere-ere-ere!*'

The Woe-Wolf looked about him. Nothing but

stones, upright, threatening pieces of rock. No white buffalo. No other wolves.

He was about to move away when he heard a sudden snorting behind him. He whipped round and leapt on to a stone, but beyond it lay only more stones. There was a sound of soft laughter.

'Who's there?' he growled. But seven times the answer rumbled: '*There-ere-ere-ere!*'

The wolf's hackles rose. 'Where are you?' he snarled.

'*Are-you-are-you-are-you!*' the answer came. But through it he distinctly heard a voice call: 'Here!'

And with that began a terrible chase after an invisible prey among the echoing stones.

The Woe-Wolf's claws split on the hard rock, his tail lashed against the sharp edges, and his ears were torn on the jagged points as he ran like a mad thing from stone to stone, for each time the voice called: 'Here I am!' it came from a different direction. To add to his confusion his own howling, '*Woe!*' echoed so persistently that in the end he was forced to stuff his paws into his ears to shut out the noise. Then he lay down panting, dazed and giddy from his mad circling.

It was at this very moment that Here-I-am appeared. It wasn't a white buffalo. It was a witch.

'Well, wolfy!' she cackled. 'Now you can see for yourself that I do exist!' She laughed grimly and the sound rumbled among the stones.

The Woe-Wolf half-closed his eyes and with two green slits stared at the witch. 'Who are you?' he asked.

'I am the Echo Witch,' she said, 'And I'm going to change you into a stone, for stone wolves echo very nicely.'

At that the Woe-Wolf laughed. 'I'd like to see you try!' he said contemptuously. 'If you dare so much as touch me I'll tear you to pieces.'

The Echo Witch shook her head, which made her cheeks flap unpleasantly. 'I needn't touch you at all,' she said. 'I have only to say one word of the spell and you'll become a stone. So just sit down quietly.'

The Woe-Wolf got up slowly. Huge and strong though he was, it would be of little use to spring upon the witch. She had only to step aside and say the magic word and he would drop like a stone to the ground. He had to think of a better plan.

'No,' he said, 'I won't sit, I'll stand as though I were about to spring, then I'll become a much more interesting stone. But you must count up to three before you say the spell.'

'Very well,' said the witch.

It took the Woe-Wolf quite a time to find the right spot. At length he placed himself in front of a big rock, tensed his muscles, nodded to the witch, and waited.

'One, two, three!' cried the witch and uttered the magic word.

But before it was quite out of her mouth the Woe-Wolf, in the biggest leap of his life, sprang and disappeared behind the rock. The spell the witch hurled at him came too late. It bounced against the rock and back onto the witch herself who with a scream was instantly turned to stone.

As the Woe-Wolf ran off he passed very close to the witch, and she, with her stone nails, tore a great piece out of his fur. That fur never grew back again, neither did the Woe-Wolf of the Bare Flank go back to that place.

Some say the witch's last scream still echoes among the stones but others say it is only the wind.

The Wolf finished his story and bowed low to King Mansolain. The hare jumped up and pushed one of his ears under the king's beard to hear whether his heart was ticking more evenly, but Mansolain waved him aside and said: 'You must go at once and get the big guest room ready for the wolf. He has told an excellent story and now I want to go to bed.' With that he yawned so heartily that the hare was pleased.

The first day was ended. On his way to the place where the Golden Speedwell grew, the Wonder Doctor had walked twenty miles. Now he stood on the edge of the Great Barren Heath.

CHAPTER TWO

The next morning the king felt so much better that he took a little stroll with the wolf in the crystal room of the castle. The sun shone in and lighted up the pots of geraniums the hare had arranged there. They made the king sneeze so that he had to sit and rest for a while.

In the afternoon he was so tired that he dozed off, and the hare became vary anxious again. Once more he pushed his ear under the king's beard to listen to his heart.

'Is it still ticking?' the wolf asked.

The hare nodded. 'More or less,' he muttered, and went off to the kitchen shaking his head.

A little later, as he stood stirring a steaming pan of sauerkraut, the wolf tapped him on the shoulder and said: 'There's someone at the door. The knocking is so faint you can hardly hear it.'

The hare hopped along the corridor and opened the door. There stood a squirrel, his tail arched over his back.

'Does King Mansolain live here?' the little creature piped.

'Yes' said the hare.

'Oh, in that case I have a nice little story to tell

him,' the squirrel said. 'I mean, that is what the Wonder Doctor…I mean, he said that…'

'All right, all right,' said the hare. 'I know what you mean. You'd better come in. Do you like sauerkraut?'

'I'd rather have nuts,' the squirrel piped and went in, brushing the copper walls with his whiskers to see what they felt like. 'But I wouldn't mind trying sauerkraut for once,' he added.

In the kitchen he had to eat with the wolf while the hare waited on the king, but after dinner the squirrel was called in to tell his story. Because he had such a small voice he was told to sit close to the king, right on top of his beard. The hare and the wolf climbed on to the bench in front of the fire, and the squirrel began.

THE SQUIRREL'S STORY

One day the squirrel Lesp called his wife and children together and said: 'We are going to move to a new home.'

'Where to, Father Lesp?' they asked.

'To the other side of the plain,' Lesp said. 'The trees are better over there.'

'All right,' said his wife and children.

They waved goodbye to their friends and all set off together. They walked all morning and part of the afternoon, but when at last they reached the other side of the plain the youngest of the squirrels was found to be missing.

'Oh, he must have dropped behind and got lost,' the wife cried. 'Husband, go back at once and look for him.'

So Lesp started back, calling as he went: 'Quip! Quip, where are you?' But there was no answer, and he suddenly found himself standing near a giraffe who had been asleep in the sun and was now stretching himself thoroughly all over.

'Please, Mr Giraffe,' the squirrel said, 'I've lost my little son. May I climb up your neck and see if I can spot him anywhere?'

'That would cost you two shillings,' the giraffe said.

'And if you looked, without my climbing up you, how much would it be then?'

'Half as much – twelve pennies,' said the giraffe.

'I've only got nine pennies,' said the squirrel.

'For that I'll look in three directions,' said the giraffe.

'Very well,' Lesp said. 'Here are three pennies. Look to the south, please.'

The giraffe took the three pennies, turned his stick-like legs half way round, and looked. 'Nothing to be seen,' he said.

'Take another three pennies,' said the squirrel. 'Look to the west, please'.

The giraffe took the three pennies and turned his neck westwards.

'That's not fair!' said the squirrel. 'All that twisting makes your neck shorter.'

'Your little son isn't there anyway,' said the giraffe.

'But you're cheating me, taking my money and

only doing half the work!' Lesp cried.

'Do I have to go on looking?' the giraffe asked.

'Yes, but only if you turn your whole body,' said the squirrel. 'I have just three pennies left. Here, take them!'

'For an extra penny I'll stretch my neck' the giraffe said.

'I haven't any more,' Lesp said unhappily. 'But please help me to look.'

'Which way?' said the giraffe.

'To the north,' the squirrel decided. 'Oh…I know! I'll borrow a penny from the hamster, so stretch away!'

The giraffe stretched and looked, and looked and stretched.

'For one more penny a little bit to the east,' the squirrel cried.

'Nothing in sight,' said the giraffe.

Now Lesp had spent all his money and owed more besides. But he knew he had to look for his little son in the east.

First he went to the hamster. This kindly creature not only had some small savings but some good advice as well. 'Listen to me …' he said.

'Here you are, Mr Giraffe,' Lesp said when he returned. 'Here's what I borrowed from the hamster. He also asked me to tell you a little secret. Listen…'

The giraffe bent his head but not quite low enough for the squirrel.

'Wait a minute!' Lesp cried. He jumped up and

climbed to the top of the giraffe's neck. 'Oozle-wizzle-pouff!' he whispered into the giraffe's warm ear, and quickly looked to the east.

'What did you say?' asked the giraffe.

'There's my Quip!' cried Lesp so loudly that the ear twitched. Then he slid down to the ground and in fourteen hops reached his child and carried him off, all before the giraffe had recovered from his fright.

Hardly had the squirrel finished his story when King Mansolain began to laugh. He threw back his head and laughed so heartily that his beard pulled from under the squirrel who fell backwards onto his tail.

'Hm, hm, hm!' the king laughed. 'Quite a chap,

that Lesp! I bet he was *your* father and *you* were the lost one!'

The squirrel nodded, rather embarrassed.

'Now you must show what you can do,' Mansolain said. 'Climb up my beard and then you may kiss me goodnight.'

Shaking their heads, the hare and the wolf watched as the little red squirrel clambered up the long white beard and pressed his whiskers against King Mansolain's wrinkled old cheek. 'Sleep well, sire,' the little creature whispered, and clambered down again.

'Did you hear his heart beating?' the hare asked when the squirrel reached the floor.

'I, I don't think so,' the squirrel stammered. But the king rose and said: 'I'm all right. I'm going to bed now. The wolf can stay in the guest room and the squirrel can sleep in the crystal room among the geraniums. Till tomorrow then!'

Thus ended the second day, and while the hare was gazing after the king as he shuffled slowly to his room, leaning on his stick, fifty miles away the Wonder Doctor stood at the foot of a giant oak. It was the only tree on the whole of the Great Barren Heath. The place where the Golden Speedwell grew was still far away....

CHAPTER THREE

The squirrel was the first to wake up next morning. He heard the wolf still snoring in the guest room, so he decided to sniff about a bit and explore the rooms in the copper castle. But he soon discovered that all the doors were locked. He thought this rather mysterious, but later, when he joined the hare in the kitchen, he could not summon up quite enough courage to ask about it. So he just helped as well as he could by toasting pieces of bread at the fire, because the hare said the king was fond of toast. 'His heart needs the Golden Speedwell to put it right,' he said, 'but as we haven't got it yet we must make do with toast.'

The wolf came into the kitchen, yawning loudly. 'I wouldn't say no to a nice little chicken,' he rumbled drowsily. But the hare tied a checked apron round his middle and told him to wash up last night's dishes.

After breakfast King Mansolain, accompanied by the wolf and the squirrel, went to one of the rooms, the door of which the hare opened with a large key. Inside, many candles were burning; their flickering yellow flames were reflected in the copper walls so that the animals had to blink their eyes to get accustomed to the light.

In the middle of the room stood a stone statue of the king, made when he was still young and wearing a short, stiff beard. At the foot of the statue lay a pile of big books full of pictures and maps of the world as it had looked a thousand years before. In one of the pictures was a witch, painted in red, and underneath was the story of all the dreadful things she had done. The squirrel did not want to look, but the wolf read every word with glittering eyes.

King Mansolain stared gloomily at the statue for a while, then shuffled from the room. 'My end is approaching,' he muttered to himself. 'I want to look at all this once more and then I'll close my eyes for ever.'

The hare overheard him. 'Oh, heavens!' he thought. 'I do hope someone will turn up soon with another story. Otherwise…'

At that very moment he heard a little voice calling: 'Open! Please open the door!'

The hare jumped to the door. 'Who's there?' he called.

'Mee!' the voice answered.

'Who is me?' the hare asked.

'Mee? Why, me, of course! Please open the door, I've been standing out here for about an hour already.'

It was a little rabbit from the sand dunes who said his name was Mee. He had knocked a hundred times on the door without being heard.

The hare took him along to the kitchen. There he was allowed to have tea with the wolf and the squirrel, while the hare went to take his afternoon nap on the king's beard.

In the evening they ate carrots and plum cake and afterwards Mee was taken to the king to tell his story.

'I only hope it's a good one,' grumbled the wolf, 'otherwise we'll fall asleep.'

The little rabbit-of-the-dunes made such a low bow to the king that his ears swept the floor. Then he sat upright, sighed deeply and began.

THE RABBIT-OF-THE-DUNES' STORY

The dunes are very beautiful. In the autumn red and orange berries grow on the thorn bushes, and then they are still more beautiful. I had a brother rabbit called Fliz. He could jump further than I, but still he never left me behind, even when we went for very long walks.

When the sun shone everything smelled so nice in the dunes. There were leaves that had a scent like sweet balm, and bushes of thyme and clumps of violets. My brother used to rub the leaves between his paws and then let me smell them.

Early one morning, when the sun was just touching the tops of the dunes, Fliz shook me awake and said: 'Come on! Today we're going to have a look at the Great Murmuring.'

Now this was something we were not allowed to do because it is not suitable for rabbits, and anyhow much too far, or so our parents always told us. But my brother was so bold that I felt brave enough to go with him.

We sneaked out of our burrow, creeping stealthily under the bushes to the top of the hill. There on the crest of our dune we sat quietly for a while. The sun shone warmly on our backs, and in front of us, far off, we could hear the sound of the Great Murmuring.

'We may have a long way to go, Mee,' my brother told me. 'Maybe we won't get home tonight, but we can easily sleep out somewhere.' That sounded like a nice adventure to me.

'Look!' Fliz pointed. 'We have to cross the valley and creep along by the bushes down there, then over that high dune.'

We started off again, scrambling down to the valley. I still remember the seagulls that were flying about in front of us. 'Bad, bad, bad!' they screamed.

But one of them laughed loudly, and that was even worse.

It was late in the afternoon when we reached the top of the high dune. The sound of the Great Murmuring was much clearer now, but there were still more dunes ahead and the tall grass that grew on them prevented our seeing anything much.

'I daren't go any further,' I told my brother. 'The Great Murmuring might be something dangerous that will swallow us up. Let's go home.'

My ears had dropped onto the back of my neck, but now my brother stroked them upright again. 'Don't be scared,' he said. 'I'm here, aren't I? I want to know what the Great Murmuring *is*. We hear it all day long. I can't live and get married without even knowing what it looks like.'

'Are you going to get married?' I asked and felt a little sad, for then he wouldn't be able to play with me any more.

'No, no, not really!' he said and hopped down a sandy path. I followed, and we continued in this way for quite a time. It all looked so different from the ground around our burrow. Sharp thorns grew everywhere, and long, coarse grass, and from time to time we sank up to our middles in the sand.

A bit further on we had to climb again, but I was tired and the sun had already gone down. Fliz tried to push me along. I heard him panting as the sand sank away under his feet. The higher we went, the harder the wind blew; the grass whipped against my nose and my ears were blown so full of sharp sand that it made me cry. But Fliz pushed and pulled until we were both on top of the dune. There the Great Murmuring sounded loud, like the rumble of thunder, and I dared not look. But Fliz did, and I heard him say softly. 'Brother Mee, Brother Mee, I see where the world ends. I see the great heaving plain that the sky bumps into and that swallows the sun. You must look!'

My brother put his forelegs round my neck and lifted my head. 'Go on,' he said. 'Look!' And so I looked.

I saw the sea and the red sun setting in it. Then I began to tremble and wanted to go home to our warm burrow, for the great watery waste and the thundering surf crested with white foam is not for rabbits.

But Fliz, my brother, began to shout and dance. 'I'm going down there!' he cried. 'That's the place where the scales of the world lie, the big white ones we call shells.'

'No, no!' I cried. 'Stay here with me, Fliz. Don't go near the Great Murmuring!'

But he went forward, and poked his ears over the edge. 'One big white one,' he muttered. 'A beautiful big white shell to take home to my bride.'

'But you aren't going to get married, are you?' I called. 'Don't leave me alone!'

My brother looked back once more. 'Wait for me here,' he said, and with a big jump disappeared down the steep sandy slope.

Carefully I crawled towards the edge and peeped

through the swishing grass. Far down on the darkening beach I thought I could see him, peering about. But at the same moment, on every side, the seagulls began to scream. They flew in groups, crying and diving over the very spot where I had seen Fliz.

'You don't belong here!' they screeched. 'Get out! The beach is ours!' Their screaming grew louder and seemed to move towards the sea.

'Fliz!' I called. 'Come back!' But nobody heard. I wanted to dash down after him but I didn't dare. I just stayed where I was and watched the gulls whirling about in the sky. Below them on the empty beach I could see my brother with his long ears, hopping about. Then everything began to waver and swim because of the tears in my eyes. I thought Fliz might be caught by the waves, so I quickly brushed my eyes with the back of my paws, but when I looked again I could no longer see him. The seagulls were still screaming, though not so loudly now, and soon they flew away, scattering in different directions.

I waited and listened, but heard only the thumping of the big breakers on the sand as it grew darker and darker.

Once more everything swam through my tears. I didn't brush them away this time: my brother hadn't come back. I thought of how, up till now, he had never left me behind, and I waited all night. But when the sun rose again on the other side of the sky, I couldn't see Fliz anywhere. I feared the waves had swept him away, and I walked all the way home alone.

In the throne room of the copper castle there was a short silence. Then Mee said: 'But at home I didn't want to play with anyone any more, and after a while I began to hope that the waves might have washed Fliz safely ashore somewhere. That's why I came away, searching for him further and further afield, until I met the Wonder Doctor not so far from here. That's my story, the only one I know, and it really happened...Perhaps I shall find my brother one day.'

King Mansolain looked up. Tears shone in his eyes too. 'Who knows?' he said gently. 'But now you'd better go to bed. The hare will take you to the room with the statue and the big books. You'll find a pillow there too.' The rabbit-of-the-dunes bowed and followed the hare.

'Good night, sire,' the wolf rumbled.

'Good night, sleep tight!' the squirrel piped softly.

As they entered the room the hare said: 'If your brother is still alive he'll certainly come this way, for he too will have a story to tell.' And with that thought everyone went to bed full of hope, and all night long the copper castle resounded with snores.

Far away, the Wonder Doctor was toiling over the Great Barren Heath. In the distance the first mountains came into sight....

CHAPTER FOUR

The next day King Mansolain summoned the hare, the wolf, the squirrel, and the rabbit-of-the-dunes to appear before his throne. He spread his beard on the floor and told them to sit on it. Then he said: 'I thank you all for coming to see me, but now you must leave this gloomy castle and go out into the world again to lead your own lives. I am old and must soon die. Goodbye.'

But the hare quickly winked at the other animals so that they all answered together: 'Oh, no, sire! We want to stay here with you. Perhaps more of us will turn up soon, and the more the merrier!'

Then the king rose so that they had hastily to jump off his beard, and he said: 'That's very nice of you. Tonight I'd like to have dinner with you all in the crystal room. Hare, put candles on the table, but first please get the key of the yellow iris room because I haven't seen it for a long time.'

The animals followed him into a room that had a floor of beaten earth. It was full of yellow irises and smelled of wild mint. In the middle was a fountain spurting water into a pool, and in the pool lived a fat goldfish that blew bubbles when you hissed, 'Bliss-bliss!' into the water. King Mansolain fed it with dried flies.

In the afternoon the hare laid the table while the wolf fanned the kitchen fire and the rabbit rolled out the dough for the cake. Quip, the squirrel, shelled nuts and made them into a wreath to decorate the cake.

The result of all this activity was a nice little dinner by candlelight with many good things to eat. But all the time the hare was listening with pricked ears for any rat-tats on the door.

Suddenly there was a tinkling of glass and something thumped onto the table beside the cake. The bottle of wine tumbled over and with a glug-glug made a big red stain on the white cloth.

'*Quack-quack!*' somebody cried, and when the animals opened their eyes again they saw a fat duck sitting there.

'I couldn't find a door anywhere,' the duck said, breathlessly. 'Then I saw a light and thought the window was open. I never noticed the glass. I'm very sorry but I was trying to find the king so that I … where is the king? I've never seen him.'

'Here I am,' said King Mansolain.

The duck, who had landed with her tail towards him, turned round hastily. 'Oh, so you're he,' she quacked. 'What a beautiful old gentleman…I mean…oh, please forgive me!' Bowing low, she accidentally dipped her beak into the gravy dish. '*Ouff-pouff*, how terrible!' she cried and blew, spattering gravy all over the wolf.

'*Wuff!*' he exclaimed so crossly that the duck flew with a screech to the top of the cupboard.

The king rose. 'Come,' he said, 'let's all go into the next room and eat our cake there.'

Soon all the animals were sitting on the floor round old, grey Mansolain's throne, munching pieces of cake.

'Now,' said the duck at last, 'I have a story the king

must hear.' She shook her feathers, tapped three times on the floor with her beak, and began.

THE DUCK'S STORY

It all happened by the pond that lay hidden in the woods. Not a soul knew this pond existed, except the ducks that lived there. White ducks and brown ducks, and they were always quarrelling.

In the middle of the pond was a little island on which grew some grass and a few bushes. Whenever a white duck wanted to land on it a brown one chased it away, and if a brown one tried, a white one rushed to prevent it. So nobody ever walked on that little island, and nobody trampled the grass flat or nibbled at the bushes.

For years they lived like this, but from time to time one of them flew away high, high above the water, circling above the tree tops then disappearing from sight. Such fly-aways were never heard of again, so in the end there were only three white and two brown ducks left.

One day a dwarf appeared on the bank.

'Hey you!' he cried in a hoarse voice. 'Ferry me over!'

The ducks immediately swam towards him, staring curiously at the little man, but keeping their distance because they had never seen him before.

'Don't keep floating about in that idiotic way!' the dwarf cried crossly. 'Take me on your backs. I've got to get to the island.'

The white ducks looked at one another and so did the brown ones. 'You've no business there, it's ours!' the white ones chattered.

'Nothing of the sort, it's ours!' cried the brown ones more loudly.

The dwarf half closed his eyes and looked from the brown ducks to the white ones. 'You're quarrelling and you don't know what about!' he cried, laughing hoarsely. He spat into the water and went on: 'You don't even know that there's a golden treasure buried on the island.'

'What!' cried the ducks, and at once turned around and set off for the island. But the dwarf laughed even louder and said: 'Silly creatures! You'd never be able to find it. Only *I* know where it's buried.'

So the ducks turned around again. 'Tell us!' the brown ones cried. But Snook, the biggest of the white ducks, climbed on to the bank and offered to take the dwarf across. Of course he was instantly chased into the water again by the brown ones, and a lot of quarrelsome pecking and splashing followed.

The dwarf took no notice. He picked a piece of grass and chewed it as he looked at the trees that grew around the pond. His eye soon fell on a rowan tree that had grown crooked and hung quite far out over the water. It had one little branch of red berries that dangled almost directly above the tiny island.

'Well, I'm jiggered!' he exclaimed. 'I don't need

you at all, you quarrelsome quackers.' But the ducks were so busy chattering angrily at each other that they didn't hear him.

Only after the dwarf had climbed quite a way along the branch of the rowan tree did they realize what was happening.

'Look out, the dwarf is climbing across!' the white duck cried. 'We must get to the island before he does!'

'Aha!' cried the brown ones. 'He'll fall into the water in a minute, and then whoever gets him, keeps him!' and they kept on swimming about just below the dwarf as he crawled laboriously along the branch.

'If you think I'll fall in, you're sadly mistaken,' said the dwarf. But that was only boasting.

The climb was not at all easy, especially as his beard was in the way. Also the quarrelling ducks made him nervous, for now the white ones had returned from the little island and were swimming around the brown ones, looking up all the time to see if the dwarf was going to fall.

Because of this, nobody noticed that there were only four ducks now. Snook was nowhere to be seen. He had crept onto the island all by himself. 'Let them go on quarrelling over the dwarf,' he thought. 'It's a good chance for me to poke about here on my own.' And he waddled through the grass and among the bushes. 'Maybe I'll come across the treasure by accident,' he thought hopefully. But he couldn't find any ground that had been disturbed, or a special stick or stone to show where to dig. However, in a little spot hidden by three tall bushes, Snook did find some strange plants. They had hairy green stems and big round buds or pods, the like of which he had never seen before. Perhaps they meant something. But Snook decided to have another look at the dwarf first.

The little man appeared to have made quite good progress and was not far now from the slender branch with the red berries. Below him the ducks chattered more angrily and nervously than ever. 'He's going to get there!' 'He'll never get there!' At the same time they tried to push one another under the water.

It began to grow dark in the wood. The sun had set and the moon was still too low to give any light. The dwarf had almost reached the end of the branch, but now his strength was failing and he was muttering under his breath. The twig he clung to was very thin and bent sharply. Cautiously, he edged a little further forward and grasped the tip of the twig. Measuring the distance with his eye, he sprang, swinging outwards. The cluster of berries broke off, and with a piercing scream the dwarf fell splash! into the black water.

The ducks rushed at him, snapping their beaks under water. The white ones got hold of something, but so did the brown ones. Pulling furiously in opposite directions, a terrible tug-of-war began.

Snook stood rooted to the spot, watching. In the dark he could vaguely see the ducks pecking and jerking and tugging as though it was food they were after.

'The dwarf will drown,' he thought. 'They're pushing him under all the time and he can't breathe.' He started to quack: 'Stop it, you sillies!' and was just going to jump into the water to help, when he suddenly heard a snuffling sound. Something was creeping up the bank quite close to him. Snook moved towards it warily and peeped from behind a tall tussock of grass. There sat the dwarf, wringing out his beard, shaking his head, and blowing water from his nose.

'*Hee-hee! Pff!*' the little man spluttered. 'Let 'em go on fighting over the rowan berries, the ninnies! Now I can get on with my business without interference.' He got up and disappeared behind some bushes, but Snook waddled after him, for certainly the dwarf was going to dig up the golden treasure and Snook wanted to know where it was.

The two of them pushed through the long grass, moving from bush to bush, till they came to the spot where the plants with the strange round buds grew. 'This is where it will be,' the duck thought. But the dwarf didn't begin to dig. The little man sat down and seemed to be waiting for something. Snook peeped through a bush and watched, his tail bobbing with excitement.

Slowly the moon appeared from behind the trees,

its beams making a circle of light on the grass. The circle grew bigger and gradually moved on until it came to the first round bud.

Then the miracle happened. Hardly had the moonbeam touched one of the green fleshly buds when, with a plop, it opened and a white flower appeared, as big as a fist.

'Ah!' quacked Snook, 'how beautiful!'

The dwarf turned with a start and then leaped at the duck.

'What are you doing here, you Peeping Tom!' he snapped, and closed his fingers around the bird's neck.

'Let go…*uck-uck*…let go!' Snook choked. 'I'm not doing any harm, am I?'

'You're a bad-tempered trouble-maker, that's what you are!' the dwarf cried.

'Not me,' Snook said, 'I was the one who offered at once to ferry you over. Then I came to the island just to…to…'

The dwarf grinned. 'To search for the gold, I'll be bound!' he said.

'Well, as a matter of fact, yes,' Snook replied.

'You would have searched for a very long time,' the dwarf went on. 'There isn't golden treasure at all, you see. I made all that up. I only came to pick these flowers.'

'What sort of flowers are they?' Snook asked.

'White wishing-flowers,' the dwarf answered. 'When you dip your nose into one and breathe in deeply, you become completely changed inside. Then, if you look upwards, you'll see that the stars are a golden city that you can fly to, just like that!'

'And is that what you're going to do now?' Snook asked.

'Pooh!' The dwarf was contemptuous. 'I've no wish for anything up there, thanks! I only pick and dry these for the seeds. I've already got a shed full of them against bad times.'

'Well, I wouldn't mind having a sniff,' Snook said.

'That would cost me a whole flower,' the dwarf said, 'because sniffing makes them shrink. They bloom just once a year too, and that only at full moon.'

'If you'll give me one of those flowers I'll carry you back to the shore,' Snook said. 'You have to go back again, I suppose?'

'Oh, all right!' grumbled the dwarf. 'I'm too chilled to swim back.' He started to pick the big white wishing-flowers one after the other, and when the last one had burst open in the moonlight, he had nine altogether. He tied them all into a bunch with a grass stalk.

'Off we go!' he whispered, and a little later the big white duck was swimming across the black water carrying the dwarf and the flowers on his back. Cautiously and mousey-quiet they glided along and saw and heard nothing of the other white ducks, nor of the brown ducks either. Probably they were sitting sadly under the rowan tree and, for the first time, not quarrelling.

Snook put the dwarf safely ashore. 'Here's your flower,' the little fellow said. 'Give them my greetings up there,' and muttering, he vanished among the tree trunks. Snook hesitated for a moment. Then he plunged his beak deep into the petals of the flower and sniffed his lungs so full that he felt dizzy. As if of its own accord his head turned upside down, and he looked. 'Ah, how beautiful!' he sighed. For instead of stars, a golden city hung there in the sky, with golden parks and golden pools.

Snook began to quack. 'I'm coming!' he cried. Quacking he spread his wings, quacking he mounted into the air, and quacking he flew round the pond in circles, higher and higher above the tree tops, and then he made straight for the golden city.

'There goes Snook!' said the two white ducks and the two brown ducks as they floated on the black water under the rowan tree. 'He has found the golden treasure; now we needn't quarrel over it any longer.'

So they made their peace, but from time to time they still search the grass with their beaks to make quite certain that none of the treasure has been left behind, and sometimes they dip their heads under water because to this day they cannot make out what happened to the dwarf.

The duck bowed and fell silent. King Mansolain sighed, for he thought it another beautiful story, but the hare hopped forward quickly to listen to the king's chest and hear how his heart was ticking. 'Hm,' he muttered, 'you must go to sleep soon, sire. I'll show the duck where she can spend the night. It had better be in the yellow iris room.'

'Very well, hare,' King Mansolain said, and after stroking the duck's feathered head for a moment by way of thanks for the story, he tottered off to his room.

The duck preferred to sleep at the edge of the pool, standing on one leg among the yellow irises. The rabbit-of-the-dunes nestled down again between the big books, the squirrel had already crept under the geraniums in the crystal room, and in the guest room the wolf snored so that the bed shook.

The hare thought about the Wonder Doctor.

The Doctor now stood at the foot of the high mountains that had to be climbed if he were to reach the place where the Golden Speedwell grew....

CHAPTER FIVE

The next morning after breakfast the hare fetched the bunch of keys and King Mansolain led the animals to the biggest of the doors in the copper hall. The key grated in the lock, the door swung open and there the animals saw a large empty room with a green rug on the floor. The hare hopped in and started to turn head over heels. He hadn't been in this room for ten years and he loved it dearly because the rug was really all four-leaved clovers. Then the other animals went in too, and sniffed and rolled about in the clover, making King Mansolain laugh. But in the afternoon he went off to bed feeling very tired, and in the evening he said to the hare: 'I'm so old I won't get up any more. In any case there'll be no visitor tonight.'

But lo and behold there was a battering at the door and the king said: 'Well perhaps I'd better have my slippers after all.'

So the king shuffled to his throne while the hare opened the front door.

'Baa!' somebody whispered in the dark. 'I smell a wolf!'

'He won't hurt you,' the hare answered quickly. 'Here in the copper castle nobody hurts anybody.

After all, that's how it should be in a castle. Come in quickly, the king is waiting.'

It was a sheep that came trotting over the threshold, and first of all she asked for a comb to make herself tidy.

'If you have a good story, your parting needn't be straight,' the hare said, and he took the sheep through the hall to where the king sat on his throne.

'Evening!' said the wolf in a friendly way. The squirrel and the rabbit-of-the-dunes nodded and the duck uttered a quack that made the sheep skid on the king's beard and land on her knees.

'That was neat!' the king murmured. 'Now do begin your story at once,' he said to the sheep.

The sheep bowed her head and waited for a moment till her trembling subsided. Then, flicking her tongue over her nose, she began.

THE SHEEP'S STORY

A shepherd had an old dog that died. At the funeral all the sheep stood round its grave, ruminating.

The shepherd made a speech and said: 'From now on, none of you must run away for I no longer have a dog to round you up.'

But one of the sheep did run away, so the shepherd called the oldest sheep and said: 'Come, put on my cloak and be shepherd till I return. I must go and look for the lost sheep.'

The oldest sheep stood up on its hind legs, put on

the shepherd's cloak and hat, and took his crook.

Some time later the prince came along. 'Are you the shepherd?' he asked.

'No,' the sheep said.

'Is the shepherd dead?' the prince asked.

'No, the dog,' the sheep said.

'Alas!' said the prince. 'Is the shepherd away, looking for a lost sheep?'

'Yes,' the sheep said.

'Tell him he should come to my palace and get a new dog,' the prince said.

'Is it a nice dog?' the sheep asked.

'Certainly,' the prince said. 'It is Miskindir.'

The sheep wrote the name in the sand with his crook and the prince went on his way, leaving all the sheep bowing low.

When the shepherd returned with the lost sheep on his shoulder, he took back the cloak, hat and crook and after that the oldest sheep told him about the prince having passed that way.

'Really?' said the shepherd.

'We'll get another dog,' the oldest sheep said, and pointed to the name in the sand.

'Miskindir!' the shepherd said. 'Why, he's the biggest and most faithful dog in the world!'

'Hurray!' the sheep shouted, and they ran to the palace as fast as they could.

'Whoa!' the shepherd cried, for he was quite old. So they carried him on their backs.

They halted in front of the palace. The shepherd

took an enormous comb and made a beautiful parting down the backs of the sheep so that they would look well-groomed in front of the prince. One after another they rehearsed: 'How do you do, Your Highness?' kneeling neatly. After that they went inside.

The prince sat in his golden chair and said: 'Let the shepherd come forward.'

The shepherd came and bowed low.

'Your sheep are neatly combed,' the prince said. 'I shall give you Miskindir.'

The door opened and in came the dog. He was so big that he had to sleep on a couch at night, and when he wagged his tail it created a great storm.

The prince said: 'Miskindir, this shepherd is your master from now on, and these are his sheep.'

Miskindir rubbed his nose against the shepherd, then passed along the sheep, shaking paws, which made them very embarrassed. After that he lay down at the shepherd's feet. The shepherd scratched him behind the ear and said: 'Your Highness, thank you very much for this nice, kind dog.' Then Miskindir wagged his tail and all the curtains blew out of the window. After that they left.

Several years later the shepherd had grown so old that he died. At the funeral all the sheep stood round the grave, ruminating. Miskindir made a speech and said: 'You mustn't run away any more now, for I can no longer receive orders to round you up.' All the sheep sobbed and Miskindir rubbed his nose against the shepherd for the last time and filled in the grave.

The oldest sheep then came and said: 'Miskindir, you must take the shepherd's cloak, hat and crook.' So the dog took them, and when a sheep ran away he put on the cloak and hat, took the crook and shouted: 'Miskindir, fetch the sheep in!' Then, throwing off the cloak and hat and dropping the crook he at once ran off to fetch in the sheep.

Just then the prince came along and saw the shepherd's cloak, so he asked: 'Is the shepherd away, looking for a lost sheep?'

'No,' the oldest sheep said. 'The shepherd is dead.'

'Is Miskindir looking for the lost sheep?'

'Yes,' the oldest sheep answered.

'Tell him he should come to my palace to get a new shepherd.'

'Is he a nice one?' the oldest sheep asked.

But the prince didn't answer and went on his way.

When Miskindir came back with the lost sheep and heard that the prince had passed that way saying they would have a new shepherd, he took the cloak, hat and crook and said: 'Come!' So they went to the palace.

At the entrance he took the enormous comb and made a beautiful parting down the back of each sheep. After that they went inside.

The prince was sitting in his golden chair and ordered Miskindir to step forward. Miskindir came and bowed low.

'The sheep are nicely combed,' the prince said. 'Now you shall have a new shepherd'.

They all waited for the door to open, but the prince said: 'The shepherd stands before you. *I* shall be your shepherd and tend you in my palace.'

Then all the sheep grouped themselves round the golden chair, ruminating. Miskindir dressed the prince in the shepherd's cloak and hat and handed him the crook. The oldest sheep made a speech and said: 'Your Highness, we shall never run away again.'

Ever since then, the sheep graze in the palace and Miskindir sleeps once more on the couch at night.

The sheep looked up. 'I hope you liked it, sire,' she said. 'I can't tell it very well, I'm afraid, and I look dreadfully untidy. I really meant to ask if I could stay here for the night...it's dark, and how could I find...anyhow...'

King Mansolain nodded, and the other animals who sat near the fireplace rustled their tails on the floor by way of applause.

'Hare,' the king said, 'take the sheep to the clover room,' and he went off to bed before the hare had a chance to listen to his heart.

While the animals slept in the copper castle, each in his proper place, the Wonder Doctor was clambering along a slippery rock-face in the mountains. It was starting to turn cold up there in the extreme north; the Golden Speedwell would soon begin to wither.

CHAPTER SIX

Next morning the hare woke the wolf in the guest room, the squirrel among the geraniums in the crystal room, the rabbit-of-the-dunes among the books, the duck in the yellow iris room, and the sheep in the clover room, and said: 'The king doesn't feel like getting up today. He's old and ill, and I'm afraid he won't last until the Wonder Doctor gets back.'

The six animals felt very sad and tiptoed along the corridors so as not to make any noise. The hare prepared the most delicious breakfast, but the king barely tasted it. He didn't feel like eating.

In the evening the animals sat all by themselves in the throne room and waited for any knocks on the door. Only a new story would bring the king out of his bed. They waited and waited, and it grew later and later, but nobody came to the door. The hare began to sob and the wolf was trying to comfort him when suddenly a high-pitched voice cried: '*Queekle-queekle!*' and a beetle popped out of the sheep's woolly fleece. 'I-I-I got a lift among these curls,' the tiny creature shrieked, 'because I couldn't get as far as this on my own. I-I-I had a little story too, but I didn't dare tell it. Now, if you don't mind, I will!'

The animals jumped to their feet, for this was indeed unexpected. The hare went off to tell the king, who was so curious that he started at once for the throne room.

So after all there was a story that evening, and because the beetle was so small they put him on the back of the throne, close to the king's ear. All the other animals were allowed to come and lie on the king's beard so that they could hear properly.

Then the beetle began in his high-pitched shriek.

THE BEETLE'S STORY

A beetle lived in a cherry blossom and always boasted about his mother-of-pearl house. But one windy day the blossom blew away and there was nothing the beetle could do but climb down the trunk of the tree and go and live among the grubs in the grass. But the grubs laughed at him and the beetle couldn't bear that. So he plodded on till he came to the brook. There some dragonflies were flitting about, so he cried: 'Hi! Can you fly me across?' But the dragonflies didn't answer and flew away over the brook, their beautiful wings shimmering in the sun. The beetle felt a great longing to get to the other side too.

He began to walk along the bank to see if he could find a bridge anywhere, but without success. What he did see on the opposite bank a bit further on, was a tree with such beautiful flowers that his own cherry blossom tree seemed nothing in comparison, and he thought: 'How happy I would be if only I could live there, but how can I get to the other side?'

The beetle then found a dead twig and dragged it to the water. Clinging to it, he pushed out, but a rough ripple washed him off and cast him up on a stone. There he stood, stranded and helpless, as though he were on a rock in the middle of the ocean.

Again the dragonflies came by, and again he shouted: 'Hi! Please help me!' But the dragonflies, their wings shimmering in the sun, flew on and disappeared.

Then an oak leaf floated past. The beetle jumped on to it, but he was too heavy and the leaf began to sink. The water mounted up to his chin, but just as he thought he must drown, he felt solid ground under his feet and managed to crawl back to the bank. But now he was as far away as ever.

'Oh!' he sighed. 'How shall I ever get there?' Further on he met the spider. 'Do you know of a bridge near here?' the beetle asked.

'Not yet,' the spider said.

'Well, when *will* you know?' the beetle asked.

'In the autumn,' the spider said, 'for then I'll be making one myself.'

'May I cross it?' the beetle asked.

'I don't know that yet either,' the spider said.

Well, the beetle thought, without a bridge I won't get across anyway, so I'd better wait till the autumn and see if I'll be allowed to cross the spider's bridge.

So the whole summer long he lived on the bank of the brook. Each day he watched the dragonflies flitting to and fro over the water, playing 'follow-my-leader' but saying never a word.

In the autumn the beetle again went to the spider.

'Are you going to make a bridge now?' he asked.

'No, a web first,' the spider said.

'Well, after that?' the beetle asked.

The beetle waited for five days, then said: 'Ready now?'

But the spider was already busy making a huge suspension bridge, with long cables and a strongly woven path. When it was finished the beetle hurried on to it, but the spider called: 'Hey!'

'Won't you let me go across?' the beetle asked.

'Only if you fetch me a pure white pebble,' the spider said.

The beetle went off to search. He found a red pebble and a brown one but no white one. Then he found a bead that a little girl had lost from her necklace. The bead was pure white and the beetle hastened with it to the spider.

'Here you are,' he said. 'There's a hole in it so you can put it round you leg.'

'Buzz off!' the spider said. 'I want a *proper* pebble.'

The beetle began to search once more and this time he found one that had a very small black spot on it. But the spider didn't count that one good enough either and told him to look again.

Then he saw one on the other side of the brook: a pure white pebble. He rushed to the spider crying: 'There's one on the other side! Shall I go and get it?'

'Pooh!' said the spider. 'Get it if you can, but not across my bridge!'

Now the poor beetle was in despair and jumped into the water to drown himself, but he landed on a twig that was borne along on the current, and before he knew, he had drifted against the opposite bank.

Almost without knowing what he was doing, he jumped on to dry land and ran to the tree with the beautiful flowers, intending to live there.

But alas! It was autumn and the flowers had fallen long ago. For the first time in his life he felt really miserable and began to cry. There weren't even any dragonflies to notice him.

'As things are now, I don't want to live here either,' he thought. 'It might be better to go and live with the grubs in the grass.' He picked up the pure white pebble and carried it to the spider's bridge.

'Here's the pebble! He shouted. 'I want to come back. May I cross now?'

The spider advanced toward him from the other side of the bridge. 'All right,' he said.

But just as the beetle was going to step on the bridge, a violent gust of wind seized both bridge and spider and flew away with them.

So the beetle was forced to live through the winter all by himself on the other side of the brook, and it was bitterly cold over there.

When the spring came, he could see his own cherry tree in full flower, and it made him very sad because he couldn't get to it.

Once more the dragonflies came, their beautiful wings shimmering in the sun, and the beetle shouted: 'Hi! Oh, please help me!' They answered never a word but just flew on. The beetle gazed after them. Then he saw where they were going. They flew to the tree with the beautiful flowers; but now he could get there too, for as you know, he was on the right side of the brook.

So he went to live in the most beautiful flower of all and was happy the whole summer long.

'There you are, sire!' The beetle whispered. 'I hope you liked it.' Then he jumped from the back of the throne to the floor and crawled into the sheep's woolly fleece, for he was a timid creature. 'You don't mind my staying here, do you?' he shouted to the sheep. 'I won't tickle.'

The sheep twisted her head round. 'Oh, all right!' she grumbled. 'But don't come up any higher than my neck!'

'*Queekle!*' the beetle cried, and instantly fell asleep.

Then the other animals went to their various lodgings, all except the hare. He kept watch by King Mansolain for a while so that he could listen carefully to his heart. It didn't sound at all good. In fact it ticked like a clock that was running down fast.

'If only the Golden Speedwell gets here in time,' the hare muttered anxiously.

But far away the Wonder Doctor, almost at the summit of the mountain, slithered into a deep ravine.

It started to snow in the mountains, making the tracks even more slippery.

'If I don't somehow find a way out of this place, I'll never get to the Golden Speedwell in time,' the Wonder Doctor muttered as he rubbed his injured knee.

CHAPTER SEVEN

It was a noisy breakfast the following morning. The sheep, as a newcomer, wanted to make herself useful and handed round the plates of rye-porridge. When the wolf sneezed it gave her such a fright that she dropped a plate on the floor.

King Mansolain came and peeped into the kitchen. When he saw all the animals sitting round the table so cosily, it made him smile. 'Hare,' he said, 'fetch me a bunch of keys. I want to see the tower room.'

'But, sire,' the hare said, 'in your state you can't climb up all that way.'

'The sheep will give me a lift,' the king said, and seated himself on that animal's back. His beard looked like the sheep's fleece; you couldn't see any difference, so that it seemed as if the sheep were growing out of the king's chin. In this way they climbed the nine flights to the tower room of the copper palace.

The wind often paid a visit up there and from time to time the lightning too, as you could tell by the black marks where it had lingered. For the rest, only a painting hung there, but it was so old you could not make out what it was meant to be. None of the

animals thought it a nice little room and each was glad when the king decided to go downstairs again.

It was a very pleasant day for all of them, since King Mansolain remained in a good mood. In the evening they had dinner together in the throne room where the hare served green peas with marigold petals and wild mint salad.

After dinner the animals sat on the bench in front of the fire. The sheep alone was allowed to lie under the king's beard so that only her head stuck out.

Then King Mansolain said: 'Now I want to hear another story…something strange.'

At that moment there was a loud thumping on the door. The sheep thought she also heard a roaring, but then she was always a dreadfully timid animal. The hare snatched up the lantern and rushed through the copper hall, and without first calling, 'Who's there?' threw open the door. There stood a lion with a dark brown mane like a ruff round his head. 'Couldn't you have answered sooner?' he roared. 'I'm not used to being kept waiting.'

The hare trembled so violently that the lantern clattered to the floor and left the two beasts plunged in darkness. Only the flaming eyes of the lion were visible.

'Come, come!' the lion grumbled. 'I'm not harming anyone, am I? You'll have to take me to the king in the dark then. Now hurry!'

They stumbled through the hall to the lighted throne room. King Mansolain said: 'Welcome lion!

Everybody stay in his place! In my castle nobody harms anybody else.'

So the animals weren't afraid any longer, not even the sheep who watched with great eyes from under the king's beard as the lion bowed his head to the floor.

'Sit down, lion,' the king said, 'and begin your story.'

THE LION'S STORY

The witch had a pump in her back garden. No water came out of it, only time. When a pail was full she took it indoors and strung the minutes of time on a long wire which she then hung on the wall so that she could look at all the things that had happened.

The witch was old and short of breath, so she hired a lion to do the pumping for her, but this was not only because it tired her. No, the witch wanted someone who could pump fast enough to squeeze out the happenings of tomorrow too. The lion was young and strong. For a few coins he filled three pails, but when he came to fill the fourth, the pump refused to work.

'Stay here on guard,' said the witch. 'I'll go and fetch my mother to mend it.'

The lion lay down beside the pump, and the mane round his head looked like a fringe of a woollen shawl.

An hour later the witch returned with her mother who pushed the lion aside and immediately started to take the pump to pieces, using her nails as screw-drivers.

'There's nothing wrong with it,' she croaked, and with a spell put it together again. Then she began to pump and time flowed out once more.

'Well I never!' the witch exclaimed. 'Come on, lion!'

But her mother said: 'Why not let the animal come indoors with us for a bit? Give him a rest.'

Soon after, the lion was sitting meekly on a chair, munching a piece of magic cake. The two old witch-ladies sat opposite him. They asked his mother's name and whether he had a girlfriend, and the lion wound his tail round the four legs of the chair and had to swallow too big a piece of cake to answer in time.

'Well, well!' said each witch-lady in turn. Then they started to talk about quite different things between themselves.

The lion didn't pump any more that day, but the next day he began again. He filled four pails, but at the fifth the pump refused to work.

'I'll see to it myself,' the witch said. 'You'd better go indoors for the time being.' She said this because she didn't want him to see that she wasn't at all certain how the pump was put together.

Now that the lion was all alone in the room he dared to have a look round. A wire with each day's happenings strung along it hung on the wall like a row of pictures.

In the one that the witch had hung up the day before, the lion saw himself lying beside the pump on guard. In the next one he saw the witch's mother busy with her long nails, and finally there was the pump working again.

'A strange business!' the lion thought to himself. He felt an urge to investigate a drawer or two but didn't quite dare, which was lucky, because just then the witch came into the room.

'Lion,' she said, 'let's go now and pump together. You work the handle and I'll hold the pail, and you must pump so fast that we'll overtake time and pump out the happenings of tomorrow.'

'It's all the same to me,' said the lion.

They walked through the garden towards the pump, the witch leaning on the lion's shoulders.

'Now,' she said when they reached the pump. 'I'll count three, then you must start, as fast as ever you can.'

She stood beside the pail and counted: 'One, two, three!' The lion at once began to pump and time gushed into the pail. The witch snatched the minutes and strung them on the wire shouting : 'Faster, faster! I can still see you doing the stroke before!'

'*Zing-peep, zing-peep!*' the pump screeched as the witch held the wire close to the spout to lose as little time as possible.

'Yes!' she cried. 'But you're still in the present... faster!'

The lion put his last ounce of strength into pumping. At that moment the witch screamed: 'I see you outside time, lion! You're there for ever and ever!'

But the lion was lying beside the pump, dead.

The witch stood there with the last minute that had come from the pump still in her hands. She strung it on the wire and gave the animal a kick. 'And you'd just got there!' she said angrily.

Then the prince of that country came and took the lion in his arms so that its tail hung down in a curve, and the head with its dark mane rested against his shoulder. To the witch he said, 'Behold one of the noblest creatures of my kingdom. He was able to move and feel and be, and now he can't any more because you have ruined his time. Why do you meddle in such matters, witch? Keep away from things you don't understand.'

And the good prince went away with the lion in his arms, leaving the witch behind with the kind of magic that belonged to her.

'A remarkable story,' King Mansolain sighed. 'I have a feeling I've heard something like it before.' He rose from his throne and told the hare that the lion had better go up to the tower room. 'Sleep well, dear animals,' he said, and left the room.

So another night passed. The wolf was in the guest room, the squirrel among the geraniums in the crystal room, Mee, the rabbit-of-the-dunes, among the big books and maps, the duck in the yellow iris room, the sheep in the clover room, the beetle in the sheep's fleece, and the lion in the tower room. But two of them didn't sleep that night.

By the light of the candles, the rabbit-of-the-dunes flicked through the pages of the big books to see if there was anything in them about his brother, Fliz. The lion was holding a flaring torch up to the painting and peering at its vague outlines. He thought he could make out a witch and a pump and...was this one of the moments from his story? If so, how had it come to be in King Mansolain's copper castle?

The hare slept peacefully, for the king seemed better. But the Wonder Doctor, in search of the Golden Speedwell, found himself faced by an impenetrable wall of rock. This side of the ravine was completely cut off and he would have to go all the way back. Maybe there was a way out on the other side....

CHAPTER EIGHT

The hare got up early the next morning to light the kitchen fire, for since the lion's arrival an extra pan of porridge had to be cooked. The sun shone merrily into the copper kitchen, and everything winked and sparkled so gaily that the hare started to sing.

A little later the lion entered and at once joined in, humming in a sort of deep drone. After him came the wolf who also began to sing, so that in the end there was such a gay chorus of all the animals that King Mansolain rose from his bed to take a peep into the kitchen. What he saw there made him smile; then for the first time in hundreds of years, King Mansolain himself sang, joining in with the rest:

'Hupsa, hupsa, hupsakee!
Who roars, who pipes, who sings with me?'

After breakfast the king thought it a good opportunity to open the garden room. They went there in a procession, the key grated in the lock, and when the door opened everybody cried: 'Oooh!'

The garden room had a glass roof, and such thousands of flowers grew inside that it almost hurt to look at them.

'They smell very nice too,' thought the rabbit-of-the-dunes. He wanted to hop inside and poke about, but the king stopped him. 'Nobody is allowed to walk around in there,' he said. 'There are no paths and the flowers would get trampled on.'

The animals lingered a little longer, then strolled through the corridors and halls, exploring the copper castle till dinner was ready. Clover salad with dandelion milk, and buttercup pancakes to end up with.

The lion licked his paws clean and the squirrel was now so brave that he climbed up the lion's tail and along his back, right to the top of his head where he sat, cracking a nut.

Later that evening, when they were assembled round the king's throne, there was a moment's silence, then Mee suddenly cried: 'I hear singing outside!'

Everybody pricked up his ears. They heard a deep bass humming sound, as though a male-voice choir were standing on the doorstep.

'Hare, go and have a look,' said the king, and the hare went to the door. There the humming was very distinct:

'Open, open please,
Buzz-wuzz bumble-bees,
Bizz-wizz let us in
Then you'll hear a din!'

'They must be foreigners,' thought the hare, 'they sing so beautifully.' Holding the lantern high above his head he shot back the bolt and opened the door. At once the singing changed to a deep humming, and in a beam of light the hare saw ten hovering bumble-bees.

'G'deevening, g'deevening, g'deevening!' they buzzed. 'We've come to see the king.'

'What, all ten of you?' the hare asked. 'Isn't that a bit much?'

'*Hmm, hmm, hmm!*' the bumble-bees hummed. 'We've got a story between us and each of us will tell a part of it.'

'In that case, you'd better come in,' said the hare.

The cloud of bumble-bees followed him through the copper hall to the king's throne. There they circled round King Mansolain's head at a respectful distance, calling out their names in turn: 'I'm Kezel...I'm Mago...I'm Rills...I'm Notkam...I'm Krag...I'm Krenami...I'm Hoog...I'm Zenstel...I'm Hakspori...I'm Pirituila!'

It made the king dazed and dizzy. The hare and the other animals wondered if all this wasn't rather bad for his heart, but the bumble-bees had already settled on the little table in front of the throne and were beginning a continuous humming with their wings. It sounded like the rumble of drums.

Then they said in chorus: 'Listen to what we are about to tell. Listen, O thousand-year-old king of us all. Listen, O all you animals here assembled. Hear our story.'

THE HORSE'S BALLAD told and sung by ten bumble-bees who each in turn saw a part of it happen.

This is the story told by Kezel, the first bumble-bee:

Behind a very thick hawthorn hedge in the country of the king of men, lies a hidden field. In it the grass grows as high as corn and the daisies are as big as poppies. A horse with a velvet nose and shoes of gold grazed in the field, but he was a sad sort of animal because he was always alone.

'What good does it do me to stand about in this tall grass with my golden shoes?' he muttered. 'Even if there were people to see them, my shoes would not show.'

One day he began to neigh loudly, to stamp and swish his tail. He trotted about, then galloped over the field, up to the thick thorny hedge and jumped right over it, leaving the field behind.

Who has hoofs of gold, of gold –
Hoofs of burnished gold?
Bur-bur-bur-burnished
Hoofs of burnished gold.

Who has a nose like velvet,
A soft and nuzzly nose?
Nuzz-nuzz-nuzz-nuzzly
A soft and nuzzly nose,

the bumble-bees chorus sang. After that, Mago, the

second bee, told what he had seen:

The next morning a messenger appeared in the hidden field. It was a swan, and he asked where the horse with the golden shoes was.

The crows and the beetles who had seen him, spoke up:

'Gone!' they said.

'He jumped right over the hedge!' said a bee.

The swan shook his feathers. 'How terrible! That should never have happened!' he exclaimed. 'The horse with the golden shoes was destined for the king. I came here to fetch him.'

'Well, he didn't know that,' the crows said.

'Of course he didn't!' the swan answered. 'All the same, he should have been more patient. Shame on him! Now I shall have to report to the king that he has run away.' The white bird spread his great wings, uttered a cry, and flew majestically from the field, leaving the other creatures gazing after him into the blue sky.

Who has hoofs of gold, of gold-
Hoofs of burnished gold?
Bur-bur-bur-burnished
Hoofs of burnished gold,

the bumble-bees sang as their wings hummed. Then Rills, the third bee, came forward to take up the story:

After the horse had jumped the hawthorn hedge he galloped on and on without stopping. He galloped over fields and through woods, he jumped ditches and bushes and even swam across a river. At last he came to a field where some other horses were grazing.

'Where do you come from?' they asked.

'Oh, nowhere in particular,' the horse answered.

'Hark at him!' the other horses mocked, and they looked at one another. 'Well, if you want to graze, you'd better go to that corner over there,' and they showed him a bare spot near the ditch. But the horse rather wanted to stay with them and make friends.

'I'm not hungry,' he said, and lay down to rest.

Then the others saw his golden shoes. 'Just look at that!' they cried. 'A la-di-da millionaire!' They made neighing jokes among themselves and went to graze a little further off, turning their tails towards him.

Who has a nose like velvet,
A soft and nuzzly nose?
Nuzz-nuzz-nuzz-nuzzly
A soft and nuzzly nose,

the bumble-bees chorus sang, and Notkam, the fourth bee, continued:

Early in the morning Hannes, the farm-hand, came to fetch in the horses. When he saw the newcomer among them, he went and tickled it between the ears and stroked its nose. 'You're a beauty, a real good looker!' he said. 'Nice and soft too. You'd better come along with the others.' The horse nuzzled Hannes' jacket then walked behind him. The other horses followed clicker-clacker on the road and began to neigh mockingly: 'I bet he'll be allowed in the kitchen! He's far too grand for the stable, that's certain. His sort doesn't pull carts!'

But they were wrong. He was harnessed to the dung-cart and Hannes worked him quite hard all day long. But it was only as he unharnessed the horse in the evening that Hannes saw the gleaming golden shoes.

'Jumping Jehoshaphat!' Hannes exclaimed.

Who has hoofs of gold, of gold-
Hoofs of burnished gold?
Bur-bur-bur-burnished
Hoofs of burnished gold,

the chorus of bumble-bees sang in three parts and in perfect time. Krag, the fifth bumble-bee, cleared his throat and took over the story:

At first the farmer wanted to sell the horse with the golden shoes, but Hannes told him it was a good strong animal. So he was allowed to stay and became very friendly with Hannes. But he was not allowed in the kitchen, and when the other horses saw that he had to work just as hard as they did, they stopped teasing. Now, when they were together in the field or stable, they were all very friendly. The horse with the golden shoes was no longer as lonely as he had been in the hidden field, and he wouldn't have minded staying on the farm for ever.

'Tomorrow the mowing has to be done, and that's nice work,' said Hannes one evening as he stroked the horse's nose. But that very night, Geg, a bad man, stole the horse, tying rags round its hoofs before leading it away.

Who has a nose like velvet,
A soft and nuzzly nose?
Nuzz-nuzz-nuzz-nuzzly
A soft and nuzzly nose,

the chorus sang sadly, and Krenami, the sixth bumble-bee, went on:

Geg, the bad man, took the horse to a lonely barn where the blacksmith waited with a huge pair of tongs, ready to drag off the golden shoes. But it wasn't at all easy. The more the men tugged and jerked, the angrier they became.

'Lift your foot, you obstinate beast!' the men shouted, and each time tried a different one. The left forefoot, the right hindfoot, and so on. But the golden shoes remained as fast as ever.

Then both men at once tried tugging with the tongs as hard as they could, but their hands slipped and they fell backwards, banging themselves against the wall.

The horse reared and his golden shoes glittered like sparks in the light. The men were frightened.

'Stop it!' Geg said. 'I'll sell him as he is,' and he took the horse to a rich gentleman.

Who has hoofs of gold, of gold –
Hoofs of burnished gold?
Bur-bur-bur-burnished
Hoofs of burnished gold.

the chorus sang in their deep voices. Then Hoog, the seventh bee, went on with the story:

The rich gentleman had the horse taken to a stable where three stable-boys immediately started grooming him so that even his shoes shone and glittered like the sun.

After that he was led to a terrace where a number of rich ladies and gentlemen were sitting. He was made to lift up his feet, one after another, to show his golden shoes, and when everyone had exclaimed, 'How splendid!' he was led back to his stable again.

And so it went on for many days till at last he was sold to another rich gentleman who led him into a great hall with rugs on the floor and tapestry on the walls.

'Come and see my fabulous golden horse!' said the gentleman to his friends, and took them into the hall.

But there instead stood a bony dejected nag belonging to the greengrocer who had stealthily changed horses because he wanted a stronger horse to pull his cart.

So the horse with the golden shoes had to pull the greengrocer's cart, and nobody recognized him because his shoes were painted black.

Who has a nose like velvet,
A soft and nuzzly nose?
Nuzz-nuzz-nuzz-nuzzly
A soft and nuzzly nose,

that's what the bumble-bees sang, and Zenstel, the eighth of the ten, told what happened next:

The greengrocer had smeared pitch on the shoes, so nobody noticed the horse any more. Year after year the poor thing pulled the cart and was kicked and beaten, stung by flies, teased by children, and slept at night in a draughty stable. He grew sad and hung his head, not even looking up when one day there was a sound of trumpets and the king's heralds passed by, looking for the horse with the golden shoes. They didn't even notice the greengrocer's horse.

The winter passed, but one evening the following summer the horse was taken to a little field that had already been grazed bare. Here he wandered about in search of a blade or two of grass and never noticed that someone was looking over the fence. There was a soft whistle and a hand was stretched out, offering a lump of sugar.

Cautiously the horse approached, sniffed, and took the sugar. Then, allowing himself to be tickled, he nuzzled the stranger's jacket and seemed to remember something.

But suddenly the stranger shouted:

Where are the hoofs of gold, of gold,
The hoofs of burnished gold?
Bur-bur-bur-burnished
Hoofs of burnished gold.

Before the bumble-bees had finished the last line, Hakspori, the ninth bumble-bee, was starting on the next part of the story:

It was Hannes, the farm-hand, who had heard from the heralds that the king was searching for the horse with the golden shoes. 'You look terrible!' Hannes exclaimed, but all the same he embraced the horse. Then he took him to a stable where he groomed and polished him all over, scraping the pitch from his shoes and giving him oats to eat.

After a week the horse felt proud and strong again and looked better than ever before. Then Hannes put a new saddle and bridle on him and led him outside, telling everyone that he had found the horse with the golden shoes and was taking him to the king.

It turned into a big procession, with trumpets and drums and all the children clashing pan lids together in time to the music. In this way they came to the castle where the king was waiting at the gates. Hannes handed the reins over to the king and everybody cheered:

'Hurray for the horse! To the king "all hail!"
With the golden shoes goes a golden tail!'

The bumble-bees started to dance as they sang, and in the middle of them stood Pirituila, the tenth bee, to wind up the story:

A footman brought a golden tail and tied it on top of the real one. Then the king mounted the horse and, led by Hannes, rode all through the town past the crowds of cheering people.

'Now I know why I have golden shoes,' thought the horse to himself, and for the first time he felt really happy and snorted gaily through his velvet nose. His golden tail was not real, but that was quite a good thing, for now it never hurt him when the street boys pulled it.

The bumble-bees, in holiday mood, danced faster than ever, their wings imitating the rumble of drums. They ended up by singing once more, beautifully, in three parts, in their deep voices:

Here are the hoofs of gold, of gold,
Hoofs of burnished gold
Bur-bur-bur-burnished
Hoofs of burnished gold!

'Bravo!' King Mansolain cried when the ten bumble-bees had finished their song. 'A beautiful ballad! Which king was that, I wonder?'

The bumble-bees answered: 'That was Bossor, king of men, sire.'

'Ah!' Mansolain murmured. 'I'd like to see *him* again. Ah!' and he fell silent for a long time, musing on his memories of long ago.

In the meantime the hare hastily listened to the heart under the beard. 'I believe it's like a rather straighter clock,' he whispered to the other animals. 'It's ticking a teeny weeny bit more evenly.'

The wolf's loud yawn made everybody jump. 'I'm for bed!' he rumbled, and fixed his green eyes on the bumble-bees. 'You don't hum in your sleep, I hope?' he asked.

'No, no, no, no!' the bumble-bees shouted. They flew upwards, each settling on one of the king's fingers to say goodnight. It looked as if he had on ten rings set with big jewels.

The wolf's goodnight was a hint to the other animals, for after he had nuzzled the king's knee and gone off to the guest room, the squirrel piped: 'Sleep tight!' and crept away to the geraniums in the crystal room. Mee, the rabbit-of –the-dunes, laid his head for a moment on the king's feet, then hopped off to the room with the books. The duck said: '*quack-quack*-night!' and waddled away to the yellow iris room. But from under the king's beard the sheep cried: 'Oh, sire! Please ride to bed on my back!'

There was a tiny shriek also from under the king's beard: '*Queekle!* I'm half asleep already. Goodnight sire!' It was the beetle turning round once more among the sheep's curls.

The lion came forward and laid his head on the king's lap and gave a '*whoosh!*' through his nose. 'Sleep tight, lion!' said Mansolain, scratching him between the ears and stroking his mane. The great animal padded upstairs to the tower room where the faded picture hung, and the tassel at the end of his tail went *bonk-bonk* on the edges of the ninety stairs.

Then the king said: 'Hare, take the bumble-bees to the garden room where they can sleep in the flowers.'

As the bumble-bees flew humming after the hare, King Mansolain rode sheep-back to bed. It looked as though he were riding his own beard with a sheep's head growing out of it.

In the far, bleak north the Wonder Doctor was wading through an icy mountain stream. He had found a way out of the ravine, but he had lost two days…

CHAPTER NINE

In the kitchen the next morning, the hare put a pot of honey on the breakfast table, but the bumble-bees did not turn up. They stayed in the garden room all day as they found plenty to eat there and had one another for company.

Each of the other animals was allowed one mouthful from the pot, though not too big a one because something had to be kept for bad times.

King Mansolain did not appear until late in the morning. 'I dreamt of the horse with the golden shoes,' he said. 'That's why I want to show you the copper stables today.'

Full of curiosity the animals followed him, the hare panting and trailing behind because the key he was carrying was so big and heavy. The lion thrust it into the lock, and all together they pushed open the enormous door.

'*Ooee!*' cried Mee. '*Ooee! Ooee! Ooee!*' his little peep echoed in the lofty spaces. There was nothing to be seen but some empty troughs and wooden posts. All the straw had been swept away. No animal had been stabled there for a hundred years.

'Shall we make it nice and cosy again in case a horse arrives sire?' the hare asked. But the king did not answer. He turned and walked back to the throne room.

'I'm sure he hopes that the horse with the golden shoes will come,' thought the hare. 'And why not?'

But that evening somebody quite different turned up. The animals were eating their dessert in the kitchen, and the hare was just taking a big piece of iced seed-cake filled with whortleberries to the king, when a fearful bellowing was heard at the front door, under the kitchen window and near the stables, all at the same time.

Everybody was frightened out of his wits, even the lion, and the hare dropped the piece of cake.

'HOOI-HOOI-HOOI!' the bellowing came again. Then there was a rumbling bang that echoed throughout the entire castle.

'Open up!' a voice roared.

'L-lion, go and have a look,' whispered the hare, trembling.

'Hm,' the lion muttered, but keeping close to the wall he did creep cautiously to the front door and tried to squint underneath it.

'Ho, there! What are you waiting for?' the visitor bellowed on the other side of the door, and all of a sudden smoke spurted through the letterbox. The lion retreated, sneezing on account of the sulphurous fumes.

The hare plucked at the lion's tail. 'W-we must open the door, who-whoever it is,' he whispered. 'The k-king says so.'

Huddled together, the animals stared wide-eyed as the lion slowly opened the front door. For the first time in their lives they saw a dragon, the three-headed dragon Breng, who everybody thought had died centuries before.

'Well, well, well,' the creature said, folding its umbrella-like wings. 'The king is still alive, I presume?'

The animals nodded, speechless.

'Then I have a bee-oo-ti-ful story for him,' the dragon said, speaking from the head that had a sweet voice.

'A splendid story!' went on the next head in a cracked voice.

'A gruesome story,' the third head whispered hoarsely, and with that the dragon ambled inside.

Staring at the six fiery eyes in the three swaying heads, the hare, the lion and the others shuffled backwards until they stumbled over the threshold of the throne room.

King Mansolain rose from his seat and with his dim old eyes gazed at his visitor for a while. Then, a curious smile hovering round his beard, he said: 'So thou yet livest, O three-headed dragon! And Breng is thy name?'

The dragon answered: 'For thee I live, O sire-of-a-thousand-years. To thee I bow my heads, to thee will I tell my tale.' King Mansolain sat down and said: 'As thou sayest, Breng, Thyself art a thousand years and more, and thou art welcome in my copper castle. To thy tale we will harken with pleasure.'

Then all the animals crept to the bench near the fireplace. Some sat on it, some beside it, and others under it. Even the sheep joined them for she dared not sit under the king's beard so close to the dragon. There they all waited in silence.

Breng, the dragon, placed himself in front of the throne and raised his heads. He turned one towards the animals and the other two towards the king. Then he began.

THE DRAGON'S STORY

Long, long ago, when my seven-headed dragon father, Flemeng, was alive, the mountain spirits held a big feast. I was still a very young dragon and was not allowed to go, but my father accepted the invitation. He drank beer from seven buckets at once, spattering the foam about. It was so delicious that immediately afterwards he gulped down seven barrels of wine. All this started to bubble inside him, and in order to get rid of the steam, he began to cough, snort, and sneeze. Now when we dragons sneeze, we sneeze fire, but the mountain spirits were angered by the flames and chased my father way.

The taste of the beer, however, was something he could not forget. That was why he went to see the witch Neshi. By doing a little magic she could provide him with the same sort of beer, seven bucketfuls at once. But she said:

'You'll have to pay for it, Dragon Flemeng.'

My father gave her some golden ducats. The next day he had to give her more, because he drank sev-en casks of beer. The fourth day he drained seven iron tanks to the dregs. After that he had no more ducats.

'Witch Neshi!' my father roared. ' How much do you want for seven fountains of beer?'

'Dragon Flemeng,' the old crone croaked, 'for sev-en fountains of beer spurting for a hundred years, I want your son's wings.'

My father flew home and came snorting up to me: 'Three-headed good-for-nothing!' he cried. 'You shall crawl on the ground for the rest of your days!' And he unbuckled my wings and took them to the witch.

Because I was still so young I was helpless, but I did manage to crawl outside and see in what direc-tion my father flew off. Then I started to scramble af-ter him, over peaks and over rocks and screes, until I heard the roar of dragon-singing and the bubbling sound as he drank from the beer fountains.

In that same moment I saw the witch Neshi. She came out of her cave wearing my wings and she began to hop about like a huge bird. Up and down the rocky path she went, until all of a sudden she gave a tremendous jump and spread the wings out wide. Up and down she went, higher and higher, but because she didn't know how to fly, at the first gust of wind the wings clapped inside out like an umbrella in a storm.

With a scream the witch fell to the ground, breaking both her legs. There she lay, screeching and flapping her wings. My father, who saw it all happen, choked himself with laughing and nearly suffocated as he coughed columns of fire sky-high.

Seeing my chance, I crept closer, meaning to snatch back my wings. But Neshi began to moan and to plead with me:

'Please carry me to my cave first, young dragon,' she said. 'Then you shall have your wings again.'

I took her on my back and clambered up to her cave. It was pitch dark there, so I sneezed yellow flames on to the floor to give us some light. Then I helped the witch into her chair, which was an old ox-skull, its horns serving for arms.

The flickering light made shadows dance along the walls and over the rows of books and bottles.

'Now, dragon,' the witch croaked. 'Come here and you'll get your reward.' She took three silver rings and put them round my three necks. 'Now you look beautiful!' she cried, and shrieked with laughter.

But I wanted my wings back and said so.

'Well, take them!' Neshi cried. But when I leaned over her to get them, the silver rings began to tighten and I was almost strangled. 'That's what comes of meddling with witches, dragon!' she croaked. 'Now you're in my power, for ever!'

The rings stopped strangling me, but every time I tried to attack the witch or to run away, they tightened round my necks again so that I couldn't breathe, and if I attempted to drag them off, the same thing happened.

So I was forced to stay in the witch's service for years and years and years. One by one I handed her all the magic books she possessed as she sat in her ox-skull chair, for she was looking for a magic ointment to cure her broken legs.

From time to time I would hear a noise outside. My father, quite drunk with beer, was flying about, roaring in seven parts with his seven voices. Boulders sometimes came thundering down the slope and splashed into the lake below. Or I would hear the crackling of burning pines that had been struck by lightning. Otherwise I no longer knew anything of the outside world.

After Neshi had gone through the last of her magic books without having found anything about an ointment, she said:

'Dragon, take your wings. Fly with them to the world of men and fetch me some ointment for my legs. You must be back within five hours or the silver rings will strangle you.' She fastened the wings on my back and for the first time in a hundred years I went outside and flew over the world. The beer fountains had dried up, and my father, the dragon Flemeng, lay dead at the foot of the mountain. The whole region was deserted, but as I didn't want to lose any time I flew south, where I sowed terror and panic among the human beings.

Sneezing and blowing dragon-fire, I skimmed through a city, snatching up as many pots of ointment as I could find. In just five hours I was back with Neshi again. She took away my wings and at once began to try the ointments, but however much she rubbed and mixed and smeared, they did not work. Her legs were no better and she was still forced to stay in her ox-skull chair.

A hundred years later she croaked: 'Dragon, here are your wings. Take them and fly to the world of men and fetch a sackful of letters of the alphabet. You must be back within five hours or you'll choke to death.'

For the second time I felt free as I flew high over the mountains, and I spurted fire up into the clouds and down into the lake, where it hissed and steamed. Again I skimmed through the city, chasing people with my sulphurous steam and grabbing all the sacks of alphabet letters I could find.

Then I started back, but halfway there the rings began to tighten round my necks, for the five hours had almost run out. Gasping and choking I stumbled into the cave where Neshi would loosen the rings only after I handed over the sacks.

'Now, dragon,' she croaked, 'make some light.'

So I had to snort yellow flames into three iron pots that stood in front of her. 'Ah!' she cried, 'Now I shall see how the magic ointment should be prepared!' and she took a sack of letters, blew on it, and emptied it on the floor.

'Agg brzm kff aiopff,' it read, with quite a lot of other meaningless words as well.

Furiously Neshi kicked the letters away, took the next sack and tried again. But it read: 'Bgg bgg frr,' instead of spelling a magic ointment, with all the things that go into it.

For hours she went on trying, and again the next day, till all the sacks were empty. Then I was made to gather up the letters so that she could start all over again.

For weeks and months and years the witch kept on at this game, till finally she said: 'Now, dragon, you have a try.'

I took a sack, scattered the letters on the floor and read the words they formed: 'Give me back my wings. Give me back my wings. Give me back my wings.'

Neshi flew into a rage, though really and truly, you know, it had only happened by accident.

'Here!' she screamed. 'Take them! Fly off and fetch the Wonder Doctor. Unless he is here in three hours' time the silver rings will pinch your throats at once and you'll drop from the sky, dead!'

So for the third time I could fly about freely, but by now I had become quite a wise old dragon and was up to some cunning tricks. Instead of looking for the Wonder Doctor I snatched up an old farmer who was standing in his field, promising him gold and jewels if he would do what I told him.

Within two hours I was back and took the farmer into the witch's cave. 'Look, here is the Wonder Doctor!' I said, but I made only a little fire so that

Neshi couldn't see him very well.

The old man examined the witch-legs, took off his cap and said: 'Honourable witch-lady, I can cure you.'

He took two bean-sticks, held them against Neshi's legs and said: 'Now they must be securely fastened. I shall need the dragon's silver rings for that. Hand them to me.'

'Can't you do it with rope?' the witch asked.

'No, it must be done with magic silver,' answered the farmer.

Neshi was so eager to see if this would do the trick that all unsuspecting she pulled the rings off my necks. The farmer at once slid two of them round her legs and the bean-sticks and cried: 'Tighten!' At the same time he threw the third ring over her head.

Before the witch understood what was happening, her throat was pinched so tightly by her own silver ring that she fell dead in front of her ox-skull chair.

I flew away with the old farmer and made him fill all his pockets with gold from a mountain treasure. As I had promised to fly him home, he took off his shoes and filled those too, with pearls for his daughter.

Sine then I have flown about over the world a great deal, but I have never frightened anyone or caused any damage, because it was a human being who freed me. And whenever I had to sneeze, I did so over the sea.

Breng, the dragon, fell silent, and only now did King Mansolain and the animals notice the red weals on his necks.

'Well now,' said the king after a long silence. 'Yours is the story of the last dragon in my kingdom. I'm glad to have heard it. You may live the rest of your life in the copper stables. The animals will show you there.'

Trembling, the hare took the lantern from the hook.

'Will you come along too, Mee?' he asked the rabbit-of-the-dunes, and took him by the paw. With his other paw, the rabbit-of-the-dunes took the sheep by her forefoot, the sheep took the squirrel, the squirrel took the wolf, the wolf took the lion and even the duck plucked up enough courage to go too. The beetle and the bumble-bees were the only ones who were not afraid, for what can a dragon do to such creatures as these? So, all in a string, they led the dragon to the copper stables where he would have plenty of room.

'Sh-shall I get some straw?' the hare asked obligingly.

'On no account!' the dragon rumbled. 'It would only cause a fire if I sneezed.'

'A pillow perhaps?' squeaked Mee, who liked to be a brave little rabbit.

'*Three* pillows!' the dragon cried. 'Of hard brick, if you please.' And with that he began to rub his scaly necks against the posts, because they itched.

The lion fetched three big stones and then the animals said: 'Good night, Mr Breng,' and left the stable. Just as he was slipping out of the door the squirrel turned and saw the dragon blowing flames over his back to burn away the dust of the day so that he could go to sleep all nice and clean.

King Mansolain had gone to bed already: the animals now followed his example, each creeping into his own special little spot.

Even the hare slept well that night for it seemed as though the king's heart was ticking more strongly all the time. He had almost forgotten the wonder Doctor.

But in the meantime, the Wonder Doctor, having slid down the last mountain slope, was walking through the dark pinewoods to the ring of the black lakes where the Golden Speedwell grew. On the horizon clouds were banking up. If they brought snow, even now his journey might be for nothing ...

CHAPTER TEN

When the hare came into the kitchen the next morning, he had a terrible fright. The dragon had stuck his heads in through the window and was sniffing at the pans.

'Well, well, no need to panic!' the monster said in his kindly voice. 'I'll light the stove for you,' and he blew a splendid flame into it so that the hare could start the porridge right away.

Through the open window, Breng was given three platefuls which he gulped down, all three at the same time, while the other animals sat indoors round the table. Slowly they lost their fear of the monster, and later in the morning as they walked with King Mansolain through the copper hallways, the squirrel rode on the dragon's back.

'Today,' said the king as he stopped at the last door in the hallway, 'today I'll show you something very special,' and he opened the door of the mother-of-pearl room. One after the other the animals were allowed in for a short look round. First the wolf, then the squirrel, then the rabbit-of-the-dunes, the duck, the sheep and the beetle, the lion, the ten bumblebees, and finally the dragon. But he was told to hold his breath.

'Now you must withdraw,' said the king. 'I'll see you again tonight round my throne.'

While the animals wandered away down the long copper corridor, King Mansolain himself, leaning on his faithful hare, entered the mother-of-pearl room.

Inside, it was like being in a gigantic shell. The floor, the walls and the ceiling were so thin that the sunlight shone through, making the whole room glow with pink and purple. The walls were lined with pearls, and the sofas and chairs were covered in golden brocade.

The king sat down in the biggest chair and as he looked round he remembered the feasts that had been held there long ago. He saw again the hanging garlands, the lights, the white roses, and pink cherry blossom. He heard music, he saw dancers: twelve dwarfs, hands by their sides, stamping their boots on the floor; twelve swans, their necks swaying, wings outspread, waltzing merrily: twelve black bears who went hopsa-heysa, slipping and tumbling over each other. He heard the gay laughter, the clapping of hands, the chink of plates and glasses: he saw his servants enter, laden with dishes: he sniffed the aroma, and sniffed and sniffed...and suddenly sighed sadly. 'Ah, my faithful hare,' he said, 'It's all over and past. I'm old and I shall soon die.' The king groped about under his beard as if to feel whether his heart was still beating. Then, leaning heavily on the hare, he shuffled slowly back to his throne where he sat all day filled with sad thoughts. Even the tastily prepared lily soup and fried carrots could not chase away his gloom.

After dinner the hare, without being noticed, pushed his ear under the king's beard. The heart was ticking very irregularly, like a clock that was not only crooked but had a spring that needed mending as well.

'If another storyteller doesn't appear,' the hare thought anxiously, 'the king won't last the night.'

The other animals knew that they must keep quiet. They crept near the fire as usual, but the dragon lay behind the throne where there was more room for him.

Thus gloomily they sat together for more than an hour, when suddenly the tinkle of a little bell sounded from the region of the front door. The hare jumped up.

'Thank goodness somebody has turned up!' he cried, and running through the copper hallway he opened the door.

But there was nobody there.

The hare held the lantern high above his head and had a good look round: still no one to be seen.

'Anyone there?' he called.

'Here!' came the squeaky answer, 'We're here, by the doorstep!'

The hare lowered the lantern right down to his toes and bent over to look. There he discovered two pert little mice, one brown, one grey, standing hand in hand on the threshold.

'We know some comical tales,' the grey one squeaked.

'He knows two and I know three,' the brown one cried.

'Not true! I know three, too!' the grey one squeaked again. 'And everybody is always *so* delighted when we tell them.'

'Well, well, that sounds just the thing,' the hare said. 'I'll take you to the king.' He shut the door and the two little mice trotted behind him to the throne room.

'Sire,' the hare said solemnly, 'here are two visitors to tell you funny stories.'

King Mansolain hardly stirred and did not seem to notice when the two mice neatly made their bows.

'Better begin then,' he mumbled.

The mice did a cheerful little skip and said:

'We are a town-mouse and a field-mouse. And now you shall hear our stories and one two-part mouse song. Listen:'

THE STORIES OF THE TOWN-MOUSE AND THE FIELD-MOUSE

'Me first!' the brown field-mouse cried. 'I have a beautiful story that is very short but all the same it can make you think very deeply. It is about a dandelion, and that's its title too. It goes like this:'

THE DANDELION

A horse was sniffing a dandelion in a field.

'Will you come and smell me again tomorrow?' the dandelion asked the horse.

The horse came back the next day.

'Your nose is nice and warm,' the dandelion said. 'And soft, too.'

Again the horse came back.

'Be careful not to stamp on me with your hoof,' the flower said.

Then the little peasant girl came along. She picked the flower but the horse followed her.

'What do you want, horse?' she said. But the horse just stretched out his neck and sniffed the flower in her hand.

'Goodbye, horse,' the flower said. 'I'll never forget your nose.'

The dandelion was put in a vase. After a week it was a white fluffy ball, a dandelion 'clock'.

The little girl blew on it so that the fluff flew about. She counted the puffs and cried: 'Hurray! I shall have eighteen children!'

Ten of the fluffy seeds fell on the ground at her feet. They grew up into dandelions that dreamt about a horse's nose.

'The end!' the field-mouse cried.

'Now me!' the grey mouse squeaked. 'My story is very exciting, and though it's rather short it can nevertheless justly claim to be the story of an explorer. Listen:'

THE ADVENTURE

In the ancient city of Dippity-Dong there lived a mouse who wanted very much to move to the city of Sippity-Song since he had a rather good baritone voice. So he hopped into the pocket of a passing soldier who was marching to the barracks at Lippity-Long. When they arrived the mouse scuttled into the general's boot which was being taken to the cobbler. But the cobbler lived at Hippity-Hong, so the mouse had to skip out and hide in a box that lay on a handcart. The handcart was pushed to Crippity-Crong, and here the mouse hurriedly leapt on top of a hat that a man was just putting on.

The man mounted his horse and galloped away. He was indeed going to Sippity-Song, but as he was crossing a bridge over the river, the mouse was blown off by a gust of wind and fell into a boat that carried him onto to Prippity-Prong instead.

Now here, in the doctor's house, lived the mouse's niece. He knocked at the door of her home.

'Who's there?' called the niece.

'Me!' cried the mouse.

'How did you get here?' asked the niece.

'By soldier, boot, cart, horse and boat,' the mouse said. 'I'm on my way to Sippity-Song.'

'Sing to me,' said the niece.

The mouse then sang the Song of the Grey Tail, and the Four Skippy Legs song, while the niece, in her soprano voice, joined in.

The mouse stayed two days. They ate the doctor's cheese and during the night they sang and danced on the table that was laid for breakfast. Hup-two,hup-two, over the jam pot and the syrup pot and the honey pot. Afterwards they slept in the doctor's napkin as though it were a bed with white sheets.

Then the mouse wanted to be on his way again.

'How will you get to Sippity-Song?' the niece asked.

'By doctor's black bag,' said the mouse.

He kissed her goodbye and slipped into the bag which lay open and ready by the front door.

The doctor had seven patients to visit. The first one lay ill at Prippity-Prong, the second lay ill at Sippity-Song.

'Out!' thought the mouse. But his tail became entangled with the stethoscope, and before he could free himself the doctor had cured the patient and snapped the bag tight shut.

The next four patients lived in quite different cities. The last patient was a very long ride away.

'I just have to stay where I am,' thought the mouse.

When the doctor opened the bag and took out his stethoscope, the mouse still had his tail caught in it, and before he could disentangle himself there he hung, in mid-air. Then he leapt over the patient and scampered out of the house. And where did he find himself but in his own ancient city of Dippity-Dong!

Back at home he altered the sign on the door of his hole, 'J Mouse, baritone' was scratched out and painted over in beautiful lettering: J. MOUSE, ROUND-THE-WORLD EXPLORER.

'Well, yes,' the field-mouse piped, 'that's a clever enough story in its way, but it doesn't give you a lump in your throat. What makes a story really beautiful is when you have to swallow at the end because of something that makes you want to cry. Now I'll tell you just such a story with that little lump in it. It's called, "The Field-Mouse", but it isn't me, mind you!' He paused and then began:

THE FIELD-MOUSE

A field-mouse lived in a lonely meadow under a thorn bush. In the daytime he rustled about among the leaves, hopping and squeaking. During the night he peered up at the moon. Peewits sailed overhead, their wings flapping as they cried their melancholy notes into the black emptiness, but the owls never made a sound. The moon was silent too. All night long it moved along its path in the sky saying nothing, though it must have had quite a lot to say. The field-mouse never slept at full moon.

One night he was seized by a mysterious owl and carried off. For the last time he saw the moon, upside-down. For the last time too he saw his lonely meadow and his thorn bush. 'Why doesn't it wave me good-bye, even with one branch?' the mouse thought.

Then his thoughts and everything else disappeared, for his world was snuffed out like a candle.

'And that was that!' said the town-mouse as he pushed the field-mouse aside. 'Those are the only two stories he knows. You don't hear all that many out in the fields. But in town, where I live, you hear many more.'

'Once I heard a story told to a little girl by her grandfather while I was sitting in my hole behind the stove, listening. It was about a raindrop and it went like this:'

THE RAINDROP

Yesterday's rain looks just like today's rain, but they are not the same drops. Once, when the Emperor Constantine was out hunting and had to shelter under an oak, a raindrop fell on to one of the lower branches. That drop was Spip. Spip tried to keep hold of the green leaf, but he was so slippery that he slid off and fell to the ground. As he sank into the sand he took a quick look round at the earth he longed to see. Spip had to stay in the ground for five hundred years and this made him so angry that he kept crying: 'I won't stand it any longer!' At length he had sunk so deep that he came to some underground streams and was able to swim to a spring. There he welled up with the spring water and so came to a brook, then to a river and finally to the sea. He found so many of his comrades there that Spip was pushed right down to the bottom where he was allowed little space.

He stayed there another five hundred years and again he shouted: 'I won't stand it any longer!' But in the meantime he had somehow drifted into a pearl-oyster that was being brought to the surface by a diver. Spip was able to jump out of the shell just in time and fell on the surface of the sea. This was the beginning of a long journey with the waves, over all the oceans and through many straits. Just look at the map: where it is blue, there Spip has been, but not where it is green or yellow and that was just what he wanted so badly to do, to see all of the earth.

One day Spip was caught in a bucket by a sailor and thrown out on deck. There he lay, stretched out flat in the hot sun. He could not hold himself together any more, so he became steam and flew up in search of clouds. The wind blew him up there and chased the clouds towards the land, where they rained themselves empty. That happened just a short time ago (the grandfather told the little girl) and the first drop that fell on your nose was Spip. But you brushed Spip from your nose. He fell to the ground and sank into it with scarcely a moment in which to see the earth, just like the time the Emperor Constantine was sheltering under the oak.

Now, once again, he sits grumbling in the ground, waiting for hundreds more years.

The town-mouse fell silent, but the field-mouse sighed and said: 'There should now be a little song to wind up our performance.' Then he said to the town-mouse: 'Shall we have a go at our little mouse-duet?'

'If you like,' said the town-mouse.

The tiny creatures took each other by the hand and hummed to find the right note. Then they executed a few trial hops and began to squeak in two parts:

Two mice
Came twice
Through the door
That makes four.

Two of me!
Two of you?
But me and you
And me is three.

Count me
Count you
Count twice
Four mice

Off the floor
Through the door
That makes none
All is done!

'Done!' the field-mouse cried.

'Done!' the town-mouse cried.

The animals by the fire rustled their tails on the floor to show they had enjoyed the stories of the two mice as well as their song. 'But I'm thankful they've finished,' the wolf murmured. 'That sort of squeaking shouldn't go on too long.'

The mice didn't hear that remark. They were looking at King Mansolain to see how he had liked it. But the king was silent and thoughtful and did not look up. So the little creatures climbed up his beard and sat, one on each of his knees: the field-mouse on the left knee, the town-mouse on the right. 'Sire!' they whispered.

Then King Mansolain said: 'Did you really come all this way just to tell me stories and to sing to me?'

'Yes, sire,' the town-mouse said, 'we did'.

'As a matter of fact, we got a ride some of the way,' the field-mouse squeaked, 'in a cart.'

'Ah…' said King Mansolain.

He was silent for a long time after that and the hare came forward cautiously to listen to his heart. It was beating slowly, but more evenly than in the morning.

At last King Mansolain said: 'I thank you, dear mice, for the tales and the song. It was indeed cheering. Now have a good rest, all of you.'

'Sleep well, King Mansolain,' the animals whispered, and went off to bed.

'Hm,' thought the hare. 'Should these mice be lodged in the mother-of-pearl room?'

But the mice themselves didn't want that. 'Let us stay in the kitchen,' they squeaked, 'under the stove.'

'All right,' said the hare, 'so long as you keep away from the left-overs.'

They promised they would, and soon the copper castle lay deep in sleep.

Meanwhile, more than a hundred miles away to the north, the Wonder Doctor was looking for the path that led between the black lakes to the mysterious spot where the Golden Speedwell grew.

'Ouch!' he muttered, for the first icy snowflake fell on his nose…

CHAPTER ELEVEN

The next morning, the eleventh since the Wonder Doctor had left in search of the Golden Speedwell, the king did not rise. The animals sat in silence round the breakfast table in the kitchen. The two mice tried to strike up a happy song but got stuck at the third note. The dragon left two plates of porridge untouched. The wolf pushed back his chair and began biting his nails. The rabbit-of-the-dunes stared gloomily at his plate. The squirrel sat with food bulging in his cheek and forgot to chew. The sheep just turned her back and stood with her nose close to the cupboard, while the duck wagged her head sadly to and fro. The ten bumble-bees clustered grumpily round the sugar bowl, and the hare silently tied a checked apron round his waist to wash the dishes.

No room was opened in the castle that day, for the king stayed in bed the whole day long. He didn't want to see anyone nor did he want anything to eat. It wasn't until the evening when the animals had already decided that they wouldn't go to the throne room at all, that the king sent for the sheep.

'Carry me to my throne,' he said. 'I want to sit there just once more.'

The sheep obeyed. 'The king is going to die,' the animals thought. 'We'd all better gather round the throne.'

But first the hare insisted on lighting a fire in the hearth because it was so cold. He asked the dragon to blow flames into it, and the dragon was already bending over the grate when there came a noise from the chimney.

'Ho there!' he snorted upwards.

'Hi there!' a voice peeped, and at the same moment a bird came fluttering down the chimney.

It was a swallow.

'Haven't you anybody at all to open the front door?' the bird asked. 'I tapped and bumped against it and whistled through the letterbox, but it remained tight shut.'

'Who's that?' the king asked hoarsely.

'A swallow, sire,' the hare answered. 'I think she has a story to tell.'

'Oho, stories!' the swallow cried. 'Amazing stories they are too, for we travel everywhere. We fly over the highest mountains and the widest oceans. You wouldn't believe the things that happen before our very eyes! That's why I came, to tell you the most amazing story of all the ones we swallows know. It's the tale of the wizard's daughter.'

A little gleam flickered in the king's eye, and he settled back more comfortably in his throne. 'I don't think I've heard about her,' he said. 'Tell us, swallow. We're listening.'

So after the hare had poked up the fire and the other animals were sitting quietly, the swallow began:

THE SWALLOW'S STORY

The wizard Traig was a kindly man. He lived in an ancient castle with a high tower in which a swallow nested. I heard this story from him. There was a garden boy too, and an old maidservant, and then of course his daughter. Her name was Hassa and she was a little spoilt because her father, by his spells, was able to conjure up everything she wanted.

When Hassa was three years old she wanted a doll, and instantly there it was. Then she asked for a little red hat for it, and a pink coat, a pair of green trousers, yellow stockings, and brown shoes. All these appeared at once, but she found nothing matched very well, so she asked for another doll with a yellow cap, a black coat, a pair of red trousers and sandals. She played with it for one day.

The next morning she wanted a doll with an orange coat and bare feet, and in the afternoon, one with purple shoes and blue hair. After three days she had a hundred dolls in a thousand clothes of every shade and hue. They all sat next to each other and were never moved, for Hassa no longer gave them a thought.

Hassa now had a balloon.

'Hurray!' she cried, let it fly away, then asked for another. She did that ten times from sheer pleasure, for again and again a new one appeared. Then she wanted a huge one with her name on it, and after that, one shaped like a mouse, and finally she wanted three hundred and ninety-six of them all at once.

It took two days to count and see if there really were three hundred and ninety-six, and then two more days to let the balloons fly away one by one.

'Now I want eighty thousand, two hundred and sixty-three of them!' Hassa cried, and on the instant she was almost suffocated because the whole room was so full of balloons that she couldn't breathe. Her nose was pressed almost flat.

'Daddy!' she cried. 'Help!'

But her father couldn't hear because her voice was stifled by the rubber of the balloons. They were pressing on her so that she could not even scream, neither could she kick herself free.

Luckily, at that moment, the old servant entered. Her face had wrinkles and folds that were even bigger than her nose, but you hardly ever saw this as she was terribly bent by old age. In order to look straight ahead she had to sit down, and as for blue sky, she hadn't seen any of that for a long time now.

'My dear child, what have you been up to this time?' the old woman cried in a fright as she bumped into the balloons. She took a pin and pricked all the balloons to shreds. 'But Hassa, you really shouldn't wish for such silly things,' she said, and soothed the poor little girl who was now sobbing with fright.

For years Hassa dared not have a wish, but

when she was twelve she asked for a horse. It had a silky nose, a dark coat and a shining black tail. She mounted at once and rode off, clicker-clacker, clicker-clacker on the road, and flopper-slopper, flopper-slopper through the grass.

'Here comes the wizard's daughter!' the village children cried when they saw her. 'Can we ride with you?' they asked. Hassa nodded and one by one took them up behind her for a ride. After that she played with the children, hop-scotch and hide-and-seek, and robbers. Hassa enjoyed herself very much.

The next day she asked all the children to come to her house. She showed them her dolls and her beautiful dresses: then they sat round the table and each was asked what he would like to have.

One wanted a glass of pink lemonade, and there it was. Another wanted yellow fizz and a straw, and again there it was. A third wanted a big coffee cake, a fourth a huge quantity of whipped cream, a fifth a chocolate elephant, a sixth a rice-pudding mountain, and everything was there immediately. They ate and drank until they could hold no more. Then Hassa said they could have one more wish, but they must first wait a little while for her father to come in.

After a time the door opened and in came the wizard Traig. He wore a pointed black hat with a green band and his white hair stuck out under it, while his nose was as sharp as a knife.

'Well, well, my little dears!' he said in his cracked

voice. 'You all want something nice, eh?' But the children stared with frightened eyes at his big black teeth. 'Come along, out with it!' he said, and stuck a snow-white hand out of his dark cloak.

A boy of fourteen began in a trembling voice: 'I –I think I would like a rabbit.' The words were hardly out of his mouth when there in his arms lay a rabbit, warm and safe, its long ears flat along its back.

Then the others plucked up courage and began wishing:

'I want a little goat!' a small girl cried, and at once there was a little bleating goat.

'I want a big kite with hundreds of yards of string!' a boy called, and there it lay in front of him, neatly packed in a box.

'I want a cart!' another cried.

'I want a big sack of marbles!'

'I want a gun!'

'I want a huge house!'

'A palace for me!'

The noise was deafening because everything they wished for was real. But the house and the palace were so enormous that the children who had wished for them grew scared and quickly cried: 'No, no! Not a house after all. I'd rather have a bucket and spade!' And: 'I'd rather have a swing than a palace!'

Meanwhile more things still were appearing for the children who had not yet had a turn. One wanted a real lion, another a waterfall, and one boy asked for a little sister.

At last everything lay around them in a big circle. But the little goat was terrified of the lion who would keep roaring, the sack of marbles had settled on the kite, the waterfall splashed and drenched everything, and the poor little sister stood there crying because she didn't know which her brother was. Then the children began to quarrel. The girls started to cry and the boys jeered at them.

Hassa saw all this happening with horror. Nobody took the slightest notice of her, nobody played with her any more and nobody was happy. She hid her face in her hands and ran to her father. 'Spirit them away!' she cried. 'I never want to see them again!' and she sobbed pitifully.

When her tears were dry and everything and everyone had gone, the old servant came to her. She shook her head and said: 'Hassa, Hassa! What made you start all this wishing business again?'

It was a very long time before Hassa dared ask her father for another wish. She was twenty years old when at last she did. She wished for a husband, and there, at once, he was, sitting opposite her by the fireplace, reading. 'Oh, how dull!' she yawned, and wished him away again.

'I want a prince who will court me!' she cried. And there was a prince, kneeling at her feet and kissing her hand. He had black curls and white trousers.

'Where do you come from?' Hassa asked.

The prince appeared to ponder deeply. 'I don't know,' he said, 'but I love you very much.'

'Don't know where you come from!' Hassa said, astonished. 'Then how did you get here?'

'I don't know,' he said, 'but I love you terribly.'

'But haven't you got a father who has a great kingdom, of which I shall later be queen?' she asked.

'I don't know,' the prince answered again. 'But what does it matter, because oh! I love you so much!'

This vexed Hassa, for what use was a magical prince who appeared all of a sudden, but possessed nothing?

She wished him away again.

'I want a man who is real!' she cried aloud.

For the first time in her life nothing happened.

To begin with she was astonished, then she flew into a rage and went to her father. But he shook his head and said he could not conjure up someone who was already real.

'Then I'll go and search for him,' Hassa said.

She asked for a new horse, said goodbye to her father, and set off into the wide world. The old servant went with her.

For seven years they wandered through all the countries of the west. Hassa met seven hundred young men, but not one of them did she want to marry. In the end she decided to return to her father's ancient castle.

But as she entered the gate after her long journey, the old servant plucked at her sleeve and pointed to the flower bed where the garden boy was busy weeding.

'Ah!' exclaimed Hassa, 'he's the very man I want to marry. He's better than all those seven hundred I saw.'

The wedding was held a week later. Traig magicked a beautiful wedding cake, the old servant stuck flowers in her hair, and the swallow sat on the windowsill looking on.

Hassa was very happy with her real husband. She never wished him away.

After the swallow had finished her story, she bowed low to King Mansolain and said: 'Permit me, sire, to stay here a few days before I continue my journey south.'

The king nodded. 'You may,' he said. 'Thank you for your story. Hare, show the swallow the highest spot in my castle, the niche in the wall of the attic. She can stay there.'

'Thank you, sire,' the swallow said, and all the animals said: 'Thank you!' and bowed to the king and then to each other, even the dragon did so with all his three heads. Then they went off quietly, each to his own place. But first the sheep carried the king carefully back to bed, and the hare asked the swallow: 'You fly so fast, how long is it since the Wonder Doctor sent you?'

'Three days,' the swallow answered.

'Where was he then?' asked the hare.

'In the wild mountains of the north,' the swallow said. 'He had fallen into a ravine. I showed him the way out, but he had already lost two days.'

'Then he'll be too late,' the hare mumbled, and he brushed a paw across his cheek.

That night the hare kept watch at King Mansolain's bedside, his ear pushed under the beard, listening to the heart.

Would the Wonder Doctor come too late? At that very moment he had reached the place where the Golden Speedwell grew, but it was covered by a layer of snow. He had to brush it away with his hands to find the little plants. Had the leaves been frozen already?...

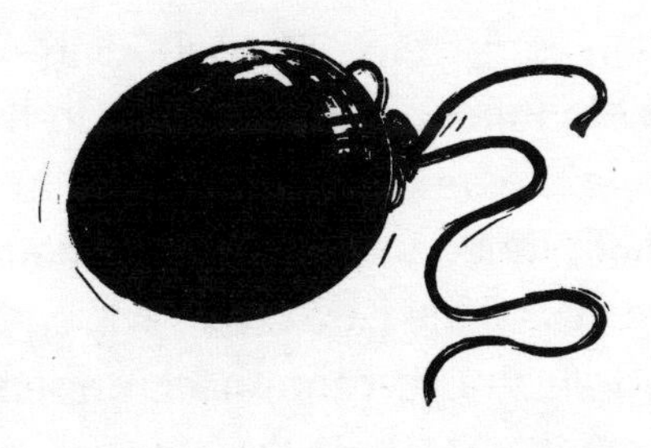

CHAPTER TWELVE

On the morning of the twelfth day the sun shone so merrily on the pots and pans in the kitchen that the copper walls reflected hundreds of specks of light. A nice little fire was burning in the stove and the porridge was simmering away so that the spatters flew about.

Then all of a sudden the lion slapped the table with his paw and cried: 'What the dickens are we doing? Away with all these doleful dumps! As long as the king is alive we must try to cheer him up. Even if he has to stay in bed surely we can think of something to amuse him? How about it? Any ideas?'

'A nice little tune might do,' the field-mouse suggested. 'Aren't there any toy trumpets in the castle that we could tootle on? Or maybe a harmonica?'

'Wait a minute!' the hare cried, 'My squeezebox!' He hopped away and came back presently with a concertina that had lain in the attic for years.

'Help!' the wolf muttered. 'Now we're in for some choral singing, just like those bumble-bees!'

The hare was sitting down, trying to see if he could still play the song of the Way-way-way, and the song of the Drum-drum.

Then the duck began to quack in time to the music, the ten bumble-bees hummed the bass, and the two mice fluted away on little reeds. It sounded very beautiful and most certainly would cheer up King Mansolain. All the morning, while the king was still asleep, the animals practised until they had a perfect performance ready.

In the afternoon they all sat round old Mansolain's sick-bed, except for the rabbit-of-the-dunes who had to attend to the front door. 'Sire,' said the hare, 'we've brought you something cheerful. One, two, three!' The two mice began to play their reed flutes: ree-ree-ree-blee-bleezybeeze! The hare stretched his squeezebox as far as he could across his chest and produced the most delightful sounds as he pushed it in again. The duck and the sheep chanted quack-quack, and baa-baa, the lion twanged the curtain cord, the squirrel jingled a little bell, while the dragon beat time with his tail. The swallow sang in harmony, and the wolf, who could not sing in tune and was not allowed to join in, held the music for them.

The woods are green, the sea is blue,
Beezy-bleeze, baa-baa, quack-quack, coo!
The sand is yellow, the sun is gold,
Jingle-jingle, baa, and the snow is cold.

We all sing ree-ree, blee-blee, boom!
We sing to the king in the copper room.
Jingle, baa-baa, boom, ploom-plain,
We sing to the king, to Mansolain!

The old king raised himself a little and looked at the animals from his bed. 'This is just like the feasts in the old days in the mother-of-pearl room,' he murmured, and smiled, so that the wrinkles made tiny new paths across his cheeks.

The hare noticed this and pushed his squeeze-box in and out with more gusto than ever. Then the mice, still fluting, began to hop about, the beetle added his chirping, and the sheep wanted to get up and dance.

It would have become a far more noisy party than was good for the old king, had not the door suddenly been flung open by the rabbit-of-the-dunes, who called: 'Look! A visitor!'

There stood a donkey. His head hung down and his long ears drooped. All the animals stopped making music and there was a dead silence.

'I thought…I thought…I wanted…I would…I really would…' the newly arrived animal began, scraping his forefoot on the floor. 'I…I… as a matter of fact, I had a story, but I'm only a poor, pitiful donkey and…'

'Well,' said the hare, 'have you come to tell your story to the king?'

The sad grey animal nodded so that his long ears flopped to and fro. He looked at the circle of animals and at the bed over which King Mansolain's beard swept to the floor, then he said, 'But…it's no use any more!'

'Oh yes!' the hare cried. 'The king's here!'

Old Mansolain stretched out a hand and scratched the pitiful donkey's lowered head. Then he said: 'I'd like to hear your story. You must tell it tonight, here by my bed. But first I must get some sleep.'

'Very well, sire,' the hare said, and the animals stole out of the room.

In the evening the pitiful donkey had dinner with the others in the kitchen. He sat between the wolf and the lion, and he sniffed at the hay cakes the hare had baked specially. But when the sheep asked where he came from, he didn't answer. Maybe that would come into his story.

After dinner the hare put some extra candles in the bedroom, the lion shook up the pillows so that the king could sit up a little straighter, the dragon rolled himself up in the corner, and the other animals gathered round the bed, the hare sitting on the trailing beard. Then Long-ears began his story:

THE PITIFUL DONKEY'S STORY

I'd always...I first...I'd really... I mean, I used to have a hat (the donkey began). A beautiful hat. That was because I worked for a poor farmer and had to walk round his well all day long; round and round and round, harnessed to a wooden beam that wound the rope that drew up the buckets of water. But the sun shone so hotly on my head that my thoughts whirled round and got all mixed up and I suddenly started walking backwards so that the water fell into the well again. But then I was given the hat. A yellow one made of straw, and the farmer made two holes in it. He stuck my ears through the holes so that it couldn't blow off. Now the sun didn't trouble me any more, and I walked the whole day, round and round and round, while the water splashed from the buckets, *sha-sha-sha*! At night I was in the stable, and when I slept, my dreams went round and round and round too, but on Sundays I was allowed in the little field, and there I could walk straight for a time.

The farmer bought a she-donkey who also came to the stable at night. She had big eyes, limpid as moonstones, and she said: 'You've got such a beautiful hat that I wouldn't mind marrying you.'

That made me very happy because I would never have thought she could like me. She said that when we were put in the field next Sunday we could get married. I said...I thought...I wanted... I mean I said: 'Yes, fine!' and all through the days that followed I thought about it. Every time the water ran *sha-sha-sha* from the bucket, I thought: fine-fine-fine! because I wouldn't be lonely any more. I thought: maybe my dreams won't go round any longer at night.

They didn't, for that very same night I was already dreaming of our wedding. The skylarks sang at it, the crickets played the wedding march, and I presented her with a bunch of white clover.

But that Sunday the farmer didn't put us together in the field. There was a low wall between us. So the she-donkey began to bray: '*Ee-aah, ee-aah!* and she cried: 'Come on, jump over the wall, you yellow-hatted bridegroom, then we can get married!'

I took a run and jumped. But I'd never travelled so fast before: the wind whistled round my head, my ears flapped backwards and suddenly I lost my hat. When I came up to her the she-donkey closed her moonstone eyes and said: 'I don't want you without the hat.' Then she turned round and walked away.

'But I thought...but I did...but I wanted...but weren't we...I mean, I'll go and get it!' I cried.

But the wind was playing with it. I galloped after it until it got stuck in a bush. It looked like a huge yellow flower as I snapped at it. But a mean thorn pricked my nose and the hat flew away. 'Please help me!' I cried, but my bride didn't hear, so I rushed on after the hat. It danced through the air like a butterfly. I snapped and I jumped, but missed every time. Suddenly I stumbled over a stone and fell on my side, which made my ribs crack.

When I got up I couldn't see the hat anywhere, and when I looked back my she-donkey had disappeared also.

I went on, hoping to find my hat, because I wanted so badly to marry her. I followed the wind, on and on, and I thought: how lucky that at least I don't have to go round and round! Then I came to a field of crows; there they were, busy playing with my hat.

'Hey!' I cried, 'Give that to me! I've got to get married.'

Two crows snapped it up in their beaks and came towards me, but then they flew round my head crying: 'Catch! Come on, catch!' And they dropped the hat. But three others caught it and flew off with it, high into the sky. I gazed after them and tried to follow, but the other crows circled round me and began to tease: 'Can't you fly, you silly thing? There goes your wedding hat! Can you still see it? Better look where you're going'! And with that I bumped into a low stone wall and the crows shrieked with laughter, *chak-chak-chak!*

When I looked up again I saw they had let go my hat. It drifted down, dancing in the wind, and I quickly jumped over the little stone wall ready to catch it. But it landed in a tree and caught the branches.

The crows had gone. I was alone under the tree and tried to shake the trunk with my head, but it was too thick. Then I lay down under the tree to wait for my hat to be blown out of it. My legs were tired, my knees were grazed, my ribs hurt, my nose was sore, and my head buzzed.

I lay like that for two hours, staring up at the hat in the branches, while my thoughts went round and round. At length I began to walk round the tree, round, round, round, as if I were at the well, but the hat never came down.

Twilight fell and the wind dropped. All through the cold night I lay under the tree and dreamed of the moonstone eyes of my she-donkey.

When I woke up next morning, the hat lay just in front of my nose. At first I thought I was still dreaming, then I pounced right on top of it. I think…I feel…I've got it! I thought. But in landing, my forelegs happened to get into the ear-holes and there was the hat, round my knees like trousers. I couldn't move a leg without tearing it. Carefully I bent my head and tried to strip the hat off, but I couldn't quite reach, and it would not slide down further than my ankles.

Then I lay down, rolled over on my back and wiggled my hoofs. Crack! went the yellow straw, the hat came loose and fell on the ground with a great tear in it.

Now at last I would be able to put it on and run with it to my she-donkey.

I pushed my head into it, but the hat would not stay on. I tried to poke my ears through the holes, but that didn't work either. First one ear, then the other, I thought. But I've got such sloppy ears that I can't always manage them, and the hat just skated along the ground; I couldn't get it on. I would have to get my nose underneath it, then give it a little toss. But when I did that, it was suddenly pitch dark because the hat landed over my eyes.

I shook it off, took it in my mouth, threw it into the air, and then held my head where it should come down. Missed it! Once more…again I missed, and again, and again. Each time the hat flew through the air, looking like a golden sun, with the frayed straw as its rays. I rushed round, holding my ears pricked as stiffly as possible so as to catch it. Once it fell on my nose, once on my back, five times on the ground to the right, seven times on the ground to the left, three times behind me, six times in front of me, and the twenty-fourth time right on top of my head.

'On top of my head!' I thought. 'At last I've got it on and can get married!' But it was unsafe and wobbly because my ears were not sticking through the holes. At the first gust of wind it would blow off.

Very carefully I began to walk back to the field because I longed so much for my she-donkey. I held my head as still as I possibly could, and went a long way round so as not to have to jump the little stone wall. Step by step I went down the long road.

'Maybe she'll help me to put it on correctly and safely,' I thought as I went along. 'How beautifully they'll glitter, her moonstone eyes, when she sees me coming, wearing my wedding hat again.'

When at last I came to the field, I saw her in the distance, *'Ee-aah!'* I called, but she didn't hear. I crossed the road and called more loudly: *'Ee-aah!'* This time she heard me and looked up. That's why I never noticed the low branch of the tree I was walking under. My hat bumped into it and fell off. It bowled away along the road which ran downhill, further and further off, and there trudging along was a tramp who picked it up and put it on.

'Where's your hat?' asked my she-donkey, but I didn't know what to say.

I went up to the tramp and wanted to grab the hat from his head, but he caught hold of me, jumped on my back, and made me walk on, while he sat on my back wearing my hat. As we passed the field, I looked once more at my she-donkey and at her moonstone eyes. She was grazing again.

'Eee-aah!' I called for the last time, but she didn't say a word.

For a year the tramp rode about on my back. After that he chased me away but kept the hat. Then I thought...I wanted...I tried...I looked for another hat but I've never been able to find one. As a matter of fact, I'm still looking for one, because if I have a new hat, another big yellow one, then I would...I should...I shall go and get married.

The pitiful donkey stopped speaking. A deep silence fell in the room. Only King Mansolain's white beard moved up and down a little. It seemed as if the king were asleep. Had he heard the whole story? The hare didn't dare listen to his heart, and he made a sign to the animals to leave the room very quietly.

They went out of the door on tiptoe, but as soon as they reached the hallway the field-mouse said to the pitiful donkey: 'It was certainly a comical little tale, that one about your hat, but it had a rather sorrowful ending.'

'Ssh!' said the hare. 'The king might wake up and that wouldn't be good for him. Everyone must go to bed now. Good night.'

Mousey-quiet the animals stole to their various places: the wolf to the guest room, the squirrel to the crystal room where he crept among the geraniums; the rabbit-of-the-dunes to the room with the books and the statue, the duck to the yellow iris room, the sheep to the clover room with the beetle nestling among the sheep's curls, the lion to the tower room, and the ten bumble-bees to the garden room, the dragon to the copper stables, the mice to the kitchen where they crept under the stove, the swallow to the niche in the attic, and the pitiful donkey...well, the pitiful donkey had better go to the scullery, thought the hare, and took him there. But the creature had never seen such a beautiful stable before, or so he told the hare.

Soon everybody in the copper castle lay in a deep sleep, all except the hare. He stared into the darkness, wondering when the Wonder Doctor would return.

The hare didn't know that the Wonder Doctor had actually found the Golden Speedwell! Twelve little green leaves, picked from under the snow. The doctor carried them in his hands, blowing on them to keep off the freezing cold as he ran back between the black lakes. But he still had to cross the mountains, and how many days that would take he couldn't tell...

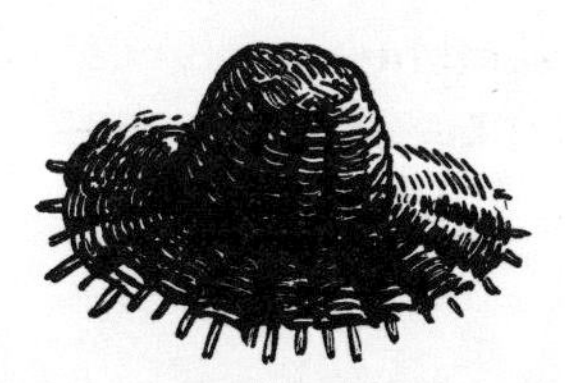

CHAPTER THIRTEEN

When King Mansolain woke up on the morning of the thirteenth day, his face looked like wax. He could only whisper, and the hare, having pushed his ear under the beard to listen to the heart, had to put it close to the king's lips to hear what he was saying.

'Faithful hare,' the animal heard him whisper, 'You must take me to the mother-of-pearl room today, for it is there that I wish to die.'

On hearing this sad announcement the animals decided not to have breakfast but to take him there at once. The sheep carried him on her back, the lion supporting the king on the right, the wolf on the left, with the two mice leading the way and the dragon bringing up the rear. Thus they proceeded step by step, through the copper hallway to the mother-of-pearl room where they settled the king in an armchair with twenty cushions.

Nobody dared make any noise. The hare was perched on the right arm of the chair, his paws on the king's shoulder, so that he could catch all the king might still want to say.

The dragon stood behind the king's chair, holding his three heads like a canopy over the king's head. The mice sat on the edge of the beard, and the other animals formed a long line to where the wolf lay by the door. They waited thus for hours, the hare passing on to them anything the king whispered to him.

'Long, long ago,' the words ran along the line, 'before I was king and even before the time described in my books – those books under the statue in the other room – the world was different, and there were stories that are now forgotten. Idur it was who came out of the fiery mountain, but who knows that now? Four books are missing under my statue, but again, who knows that?'

The king's mind is wandering, the animals thought. The hare could scarcely hear the heart beating. Even if the Wonder Doctor came this very moment with the Golden Speedwell, it would be too late. There still wouldn't be enough time to prepare the medicine.

A deathly silence fell in the mother-of-pearl room, but suddenly the wolf pricked up his ears. He whispered something to the sheep who passed it on to the squirrel, and the squirrel to the lion, the lion to the swallow, the swallow to the pitiful donkey, the pitiful donkey to the rabbit-of-the-dunes who passed it on to the duck, and the duck to the mice, and the mice to the bumble-bees who hummed it into the hare's ears: 'There's a knocking at the door!'

Like lightning the hare jumped from the chair, and rushing from the room and through the hall, bumped his head on the front door as he dragged it open. There stood a dwarf. 'Who...what...have you got the Golden Speedwell?' the hare cried feverishly.

'Golden Speedwell nothing!' the dwarf answered gruffly. 'You'd better take me to the king. I've got something for him. And do stop your whiskers trembling!'

Only then did the hare notice the sack the dwarf was carrying on his back. 'What's in that?' he wanted to know.

But the dwarf didn't answer and stomped on into the copper hall. At the door of the mother-of-pearl room he stopped for a moment, raising his white eyebrows as he looked at the long line of animals. Then he went to the armchair and, slipping the sack from his back, took off his cap and bowed low to King Mansolain.

'Sire,' he said solemnly, 'I bring back to you what long ago was taken by Idur.'

On hearing this name, King Mansolain opened his eyes. He seemed to gather new life as he watched the dwarf take from the sack four old, yellowing and tattered books. A sigh made his long white beard stir, and the animals heard him whisper: 'The empty places under my statue! Now they will be filled again. The most ancient stories are back once more. Let us hear them, dwarf.'

'*Hm?*' growled the dwarf. 'What now? What is it you want?'

The hare plucked at his sleeve: 'The king is very ill and can't read any more. You'll have to read the books to him. It might save his life.'

The dwarf looked at all the animals. They nodded silently and moved into a circle as the hare pushed forward a four-legged stool.

'Well,' the little man growled again, 'if you must hear it, it's the History of the Dwarfs, so we'd better begin with Book One.'

He took the oldest of the books from the floor and, opening it carefully, put it on his knees and began to read:

THE FOUR ANCIENT BOOKS OF THE DWARFS

BOOK ONE: THE OLDEST HISTORY

The kingdom of the dwarfs lies underneath the earth. There the dwarfs dug for gold, silver, and copper which they fashioned into beautiful objects, using the furnaces of the volcanoes. But one of the volcanoes became extinct, and a quarrel arose among the silversmiths over the use of the remaining furnaces. So then Idur decided to take with him a hundred and twenty dwarfs and climb with them up through the cooling volcano and go and live on the earth.

'You'll shrink in the sunlight,' the others prophesied. But Idur took twelve of the most delicately made hammers from his kingdom, and went on his way.

For five days they climbed up among the blackened stones and reached the summit during the night.

'They haven't got anything like that down there,' said Idur, pointing out to the dwarfs the starry sky. 'Those golden glitters tell a wonderful story,' he went on. 'Every night throughout the year they turn and travel around. The Golden Wagon in the north, the Silver Swan over our heads, and the Copper Lion in the south. But the Moon goes her own way: some say that during the summer she tries to jump on the Wagon for a ride, but she never can. And the Sun chases all of them away when he comes each morning. At the end of the summer he rides on the Copper Lion, but we can't see him doing that.'

While Idur told the dwarfs all this as they sat on the slope of the volcano, it grew lighter and lighter till the sun rose like a round window in a fiery furnace.

Then they became afraid of being shrunk, but Idur stopped those who wanted to run back into the mountain, saying they had only to go down the slope and seek some shade.

Thus the dwarfs took possession of the region around the dead volcano. They planted woods, dug out lakes, sowed grasses and finally began to work with Idur's delicately made hammers, fashioning beautiful objects out of stone. Then they built a city on the shores of the biggest lake, a city of dwarf towers and dwarf arches, and they called the city Aradabar.

Many, many years passed, until one day Goror, the dwarf, climbed up from the kingdom-under-the-earth to find out what had happened to Idur and his hundred and twenty. When he saw the woods and lakes and the city of Aradabar, and the artfully fashioned stones which glittered in the sunlight, he grew very jealous.

He rushed down the slope, his footsteps leaving a trail of yellow sulphur. He tore up two trees and hurled them into the lake. Then he robbed the city of a precious blue stone and sneaked back with it to his own kingdom.

But Idur's dwarfs followed his sulphurous tracks down through the dead volcano and snatched back the precious blue stone, and a great quantity of finely wrought gold and silver, which they cemented firmly into their city walls.

Goror was furious and demanded it all back. He appeared at the top of the volcano with twenty of his dwarfs. Idur went out to meet him with fifty men of his own, and a terrible battle ensued. Heavy boulders came thundering down the slope, crushing many on Idur's side. But with long poles Goror's dwarfs were hurled back, one by one, into the crater's mouth and dropped dead into their own kingdom.

Then Goror fled down among the blackened stones to assemble a greater army which would conquer the dwarfs outside. But Idur and his followers wove a net of gold thread which they stretched over the mouth of the mountain. So when Goror climbed up again, he was caught like a fish in the net and was strangled. His dwarf army did not want to fight any more and the war ended.

Idur buried his dead in a field next to the wood: the grass there was never cut again and grew as tall as a giraffe's neck!

The city of Aradabar grew bigger and bigger, and ever more splendid, and arching over it the dwarfs built a great rainbow of glittering stones, red, orange, yellow, green, blue, purple and violet. When the sun shone on it, it could be seen from far off. They also made fountains, and when the water spurted upwards the wind took the drops and blew them into letters in the sky, so that one could read the stories that otherwise are only whispered by the trees. And the fame of all this was spread abroad by the birds.

Now it happened that a sulphurous smoke began to rise out of the mountain, three clouds of it a day. This surprised Idur and he went to investigate. The gold of the net looked as if it had just been polished and was still stretched tightly across the crater, but underneath, on a jutting stone, sat a dwarf.

'Great Idur,' he said, 'we of the Inside Kingdom wish to have peaceful dealings with you dwarfs of the Outside Kingdom. Nemosh, who now reigns over us, has sent me to ask you to draw up the net.'

Idur thought for a while, then he said: 'Let Nemosh come here tomorrow and let him prove to me that there will indeed be peace.'

The next day Nemosh appeared, stout of figure, red of beard. 'Great Idur,' he said, 'I beg you to look at this,' and he held out a diamond saw. 'This tool has been lately fashioned and with it we can saw the net apart.' He put the saw to the mesh and with seven strokes he severed one golden threat. 'See, now I surrender it to you,' he said, 'to prove that we do not wish to use force. Pray accept it.'

He put the saw through the net and Idur took it. It was a masterpiece. Another such as this could not possibly exist.

'Was it you who made it?' Idur asked Nemosh.

The red-bearded dwarf nodded.

'Well then,' Idur said, 'tomorrow at noon, when the sun is highest in the heavens and the stone rainbow stands glittering over Aradabar, the net shall be drawn up. Then you, Nemosh, and any dwarfs who wish, may enter my kingdom.'

Then Idur bent down, and the dwarf of the Outside Kingdom and the dwarf of the Inside Kingdom shook hands to seal the peace. After that Idur walked back along the field of the giraffe-neck grass to the city of Aradabar to prepare a welcome for the under-earth dwarfs. End of the First Book.

THE SECOND BOOK: IDUR AND NEMOSH

Eighty-four under-earth dwarfs accompanied Nemosh to Aradabar. Their entry was celebrated with much applause and embracing. They brought jewellery of gold and silver and copper, they kissed the Blue Stone, they dipped their caps in the water of the lake and they went through the streets of Aradabar to see how everything had been made. After that they all held a feast of celebration and finally lay down to sleep in an enormous circle.

The next day Nemosh said to Idur: 'Your kingdom is splendid, and most masterly your city, but it will only be dazzling with the addition of our gold, silver and copper.'

Idur answered: 'Let us make *one* kingdom of under-the-earth and on-top-of-the-earth, and Aradabar will be the city of all dwarfs, made equally of stone, gold, silver and copper.'

So from that time Idur and Nemosh together reigned over the New Kingdom of the Dwarfs. A great stairway was hewn in the extinct fire-mountain as a highway from the Outside Kingdom to the Inside Kingdom. Over the years it was used by countless dwarfs as they collected rich metals or rare stones.

A black cauldron was placed on the top of a tower so that molten copper could be poured down to make street cobbles. A silver tower was also built, even higher than the many-hued stone arc, and on top of it was fixed a golden sun that made the moonlight splinter into a thousand sparkles at night.

New lakes were dug, bigger woods were planted, and Aradabar was completely encircled by a golden wall.

Thus the Kingdom of the Dwarfs existed in peace and brilliance for countless years; but then the beauty of the countryside began to attract the attention of the animals. They started to assemble at the borders: the wolves in the north, the lions in the south, the creepy-crawlies and the hoppers in the east, and the winged ones in the west. The dwarfs wanted to surround their kingdom with golden nets but Idur and Nemosh forbade it. 'Let them come and live in peace among us,' they said. 'Each kind of animal should send an ambassador so that we can show him where they should live.'

So then the animals, four-legged, creepy-crawly, hoppers, roarers, flyers, barkers, mooers, long-necked, long-haired, curly-haired, no-haired, all came to Aradabar, one of each kind, walking through the copper streets to the silver tower where they were received by Idur and Nemosh.

'See,' the two dwarfs said to the lion, 'the field of Idur is yours and for your kind,' and they put a golden collar round the lion's neck. 'See,' they said to the wolf, 'the plain of Erda is for you and your kind,' and the wolf was also give a golden collar. Thus all the animals had a region allotted to them, and each of them received a golden collar. At last they all bowed low to the two dwarfs and departed, each kind to fetch their counterparts, and came back to live in their own places in the Kingdom of the Dwarfs.

But the sheep had made no move and now said: 'My sheep-fellows and I have someone else with us. A shepherd who has followed us.'

'What is a shepherd?' Nemosh asked.

'It's a human,' the sheep answered. 'He's still very young.'

'Let him come,' said Idur.

Thus Man made his appearance in the Kingdom of the dwarfs. A little boy, scarcely eleven years old, his bare feet padding on the copper cobbles of the streets of Aradabar. He had no father or mother, so he was quite content to stay with the dwarfs in their beautiful city.

In the years that followed, the dwarfs toiled up and down the stony stairway, in and out of the extinct fire-mountain collecting more and more copper and silver and gold, and fashioning more and more stones. The animals lived in the woods and fields and along the shores of the lakes, and the boy learned dwarf-wisdom and grew tall, until Idur and Nemosh saw that he had become taller than they were themselves.

In those days the Time-Tellers came, saying that the curve of the sun was beginning to sink into the earth: 'Three inches every year,' they said, 'the sun sinks lower. Its shining grows less and so does its warmth.'

Alarm at this news started among the animals. Birds began to leave, and some of the four-footed animals followed.

'In the south the sun is warmer,' was the word that was passed round.

Idur climbed the silver tower and looked at the stars in the dark sky just as he had when he first came out of the mountain.

He noticed that the Copper Lion had walked further south, and the Silvery Swan no longer flew above his head, while the golden Star-Wagon stayed higher in the sky than before. Then the stars disappeared behind some clouds that were coming up as the first snow fell on the Kingdom of the Dwarfs and their beautiful city of Aradabar.

'Let's go back to under-the-earth, for here we'll die in the white cold,' Idur said. So the dwarfs began to pull down the golden wall, the dwarf archways and the dwarf towers and the houses of their city, in order to carry them in pieces down the stony stairway to under-the-earth and there to build them up again.

This work was almost finished and only the stone rainbow, the silver tower with the golden sun, and the copper streets were still left in the Outside Kingdom, when the disastrous snow-fall came: Nemosh and most of the dwarfs were down in the Inside Kingdom. But Idur was outside. With the boy and the last of the seventeen dwarfs he was climbing the cold fire-mountain when all of a sudden the swirling white snow enveloped them. They were blinded and the stony stairway vanished under their feet. Slithering and slipping, they were forced to retreat as huge avalanches of snow thundered into the mouth of the mountain.

The entrance to the Inside Kingdom was blocked for ever. End of the Second Book.

THE THIRD BOOK: THE ICE WINTER

The whirling snow fell so thickly on the mountain slope that Idur and the seventeen dwarfs were stuck fast in it. They would have been buried and frozen still like snowmen had not the boy, now grown taller than the dwarfs, taken them by the hand and led them in a string towards the silver tower. When they arrived there, icicles hung from their fingers and noses, but once inside they warmed themselves at the fire, though it took them three days to thaw.

The snowstorm died down and all around was silence. Idur said: 'Boy-of-men, go and look outside.'

The boy left the silver tower and saw that the snow had fallen thickly everywhere, only the copper streets were swept clean by the wind. Then the dwarfs went outside too and looked round at their kingdom. The woods were white, as if each tree wore a freshly starched shirt; the lakes were frozen into stone-hard black ice, and the once grassy fields were now giants' white handkerchiefs.

The sun came out but didn't rise higher than about five inches above the horizon where it hung like a huge red ball. It cast a rosy glow over the white kingdom and made the icicles on the stone rainbow sparkle. Then Idur saw the fountain. The last words that the wind had written with drops of water hung, stiffly frozen, in mid-air. 'Prosempl Nemosh,' they read, which means, 'Farewell, Nemosh.'

The dwarf began to weep: 'I want to die here,' he sobbed. 'Here in the frozen glory of the Outside Kingdom, in the remains of Aradabar, my city, for Nemosh is down there in the Inside Kingdom and I shall never see him again!'

But the head wolf with the golden collar came to him and said: 'The animals of your kingdom have decided to travel south where the warmth of the sun has gone. We shall not abandon you, who have been our king. We shall take you on our backs.'

But Idur answered: 'Our kingdom is here and under-the-earth, not in the south.'

Then the head wolf said: 'In the south we shall establish a kingdom of animals and you shall be our king. From the copper cobbles of Aradabar we will build you a castle to live in and share with the dwarfs. The boy-of-men is coming with us to be our guide.'

So then Idur agreed and the great exodus began. The boy walked in front, plodding through the snow, making a path along which the thousands of animals pushed in a long column, every one holding a copper cobble in its mouth. At the rear trotted seventeen wolves each with a dwarf on its back. Last of all came the head wolf with the golden collar. On his back sat Idur the wrong way round, so that he could gaze at the slowly disappearing beauty of the many-hued rainbow, the golden sun on the top of the tower, the last icy message of the fountain, all that remained of his city of Aradabar. 'Prosempl Nemosh!' he whispered, while the tears on his cheeks turned to ice.

For days and weeks and months they marched on, blinded by snow, lashed by icy rain. Many animals and two dwarfs fell in a battle with the Frightful Frog, who was killed in the end by the boy-of-men. But gradually the sun was rising higher above the horizon, the snow was thinning and at last they reached the warm south where the Copper Lion shone right overhead at night. There the twelve remaining dwarfs built a copper castle under Idur's direction. They used the street cobbles that the animals had carried on their journey from Aradabar, and they made the rooms and halls as big as if they were meant for the boy-of-men. There were so many cobbles left over that they were able to make copper mountains around the castle.

Then Idur said: 'The kingdom of the animals shall be in the copper mountains that surround the castle. Inside the castle the king will live, but it will not be Idur. You must choose another.'

The animals cried; 'The brave one who led us to this spot, who fought our battles and who slew the Frightful Frog, he shall be our king!'

The boy-of-men came forward, his head crowned with the golden jewel of Aradabar, and was made King of All the Animals and of the dwarfs-on-top-of-the-earth, and they called him 'Mansolain', which means, 'He who led us here.' End of the Third Book.

THE FOURTH BOOK: PROPHECIES

In the middle of the castle the dwarfs had made a room of mother-of-pearl. The young King Mansolain, Idur and his twelve dwarfs, the head wolf and the other animals with golden collars assembled there to hold a big feast. They lit white candles and drank red wine. 'Hurray for the dwarfs and all the animals!'

They did a donkey dance, the dwarfs sang the twelve-hammer song and the animals recited the Ballad of the Snow-Lion. But Idur was sad, and King Mansolain asked him why he didn't want to be king any longer, and why he didn't join in the singing.

Idur answered: 'It is because of Nemosh that I grieve. Aradabar lies under a hundred ells of snow. A hundred ells of snow cover the stony stairway and a snow-lid keeps the entrance to the fire-mountain, to our Inside Kingdom, shut. But we want, the twelve dwarfs and I, to go in search of another entrance to the Inside Kingdom. We will not stay here, the twelve dwarfs and I, but will wander far afield to the snow borders, over mountains, in caves, and through valleys. For we do not want to stay where Nemosh and the others are not.'

Then Mansolain was sad too, because he did not wish to be left alone in the copper castle. But Idur said: 'You will see us from time to time. The animals with the golden collars shall stay in the castle with you and form your court. And in addition,' the dwarf went on,' I shall give you a long life. Far longer than an ordinary man's, though not so long as a dwarf's. Count the candles that burn in the mother-of-pearl room. So many years your life shall last.'

Mansolain counted, the animals counted, and there were a thousand candles.

Then all of a sudden the dwarf, Anor, rose from his seat. Everyone fell silent as a strange light shone from his eyes and he saw into the future. He began to sing hoarsely but very softly, all on one note, his eyes staring upwards: 'I see the Copper Lion. It has returned and shines right overhead at Aradabar. The snow is turned to water, the water to steam. The entrance to the mountain is free. I see dwarfs. They go in and out but I do not know them. I see the blue sea. I see the copper mountains and the copper castle too. An old, old king with a thousand wrinkles and a long white beard. He is alone. He is sleeping. Or is he dead? I see black lakes. A man is hastening along their shores, his hands cupped like a ball. He is carrying something precious. I hear a ticking noise. It is an old, old clock. *Tick-tock, tick-tock-tick*. It echoes through the copper hallways. Life returns to the deserted castle. I see animals, new animals. A lion, a rabbit, a wolf, and a very ancient three-headed dragon. The old king sleeps. I see a thousand candles burning. A thousand years of life. The hall is full of animals, full of music. It is a feast. But one candle has yet to come. When one candle is brought in still burning, there will be another thousand years of life. I see a door opening, but...'

As he uttered these last words Anor's voice faltered. He rubbed his eyes and shook his head, then slowly sat down. The vision of the future had become dark and he could see no more.

The animals with the golden collars, the young

king and the other dwarfs remained silent for they had not understood very much of what had been said. Were not a thousand years enough? And where could that final candle come from?

At last Idur said: 'Let us end this feast. Farewell, Mansolain, king of all animals and of us dwarfs so long as we are in your kingdom. Farewell! Rule with wisdom and justice, and may peace reign in your copper castle. Let no animal within these walls ever do harm to any other animal.'

Then all the dwarfs departed to wander over the earth as far as the borders of the snow, looking for another entrance to the Inside Kingdom where Nemosh and the others dwelt. There were thirteen of them, searching the mountains, the caves and the valleys, but no man has ever seen them. End of the Fourth Book.

The dwarf ended his reading. He piled the four books on the floor at the old king's feet. The room was in half darkness because almost all of the candles had burnt out. How much time had passed since the dwarf began to read? One day? Five days? The hare started to his feet and hurried to the big chair. Was King Mansolain asleep or…or…? He pushed his ear under the beard to listen, while all the animals held their breath.

But who had kept watch at the front door all this time? Or who had even pricked up his ears to listen? Nobody. Not one of the animals had heard any knocking, and none of them noticed a fumbling noise at the kitchen window. Nobody actually saw the dark figure climb inside, then look in the cupboards, blow up the fire, light a smoking candle and fill a little black pan with water to prepare some brew or other. All the animals had their attention on King Mansolain, there in the mother-of-pearl room.

'He is dying,' the hare whispered. 'It's all been for nothing. The thousand years have passed and the Wonder Doctor is too late.' The animal began to sob. 'The Golden Speedwell could have save him, but...'

At that very moment the door of the mother-of-pearl room opened and a dark figure stepped inside. He carried a tray on which a black pan was simmering over a flaring, smoking flame.

The dwarf gave a shout. 'The...the lighted candle!' he cried hoarsely. 'The lighted candle comes into the room just as it has been said in the book of prophecies!'

But the hare leapt to his feet and ran to the figure.

'Wonder Doctor!' he cried. 'Quick, quick, the Golden Speedwell!'

The Wonder Doctor smiled and placed the tray next to the king's chair. 'It is indeed the Golden Speedwell,' he said, 'And with it I have prepared a potion in the kitchen because nobody opened the front door when I knocked.'

With a spoon he carefully poured some of the potion between the lips of the dying man. King Mansolain sighed, then sighed again. Three spoonfuls of the infusion were given him. Then the Wonder Doctor whispered: 'Better leave him alone now. He must sleep.'

All the animals stole out of the room on the very tips of their toes. The sheep even slid along on his woollen stomach so as to make no noise.

The Wonder Doctor had arrived in time. King Mansolain was saved.

CHAPTER FOURTEEN

The next evening King Mansolain was back in the throne room and on his throne. The hare stood close to him, one ear under the beard, nodding contentedly. 'It's regular again,' he said solemnly, 'and it ticks like a new clock, just as it used to.'

The animals sat round the throne, the three-headed dragon stood behind it, and the sheep was lying on the long, white beard that spread about the king's feet like a rug. The dwarf sat on the bench near the fireplace, and the Wonder Doctor on a chair opposite the throne.

Then King Mansolain said: 'I thank you, all animals, for coming here. Your stories have saved me. I thank the hare for his good care of me [the hare smoothed his whiskers], and I thank the dwarf for returning the four old books [the dwarf mumbled in his beard]. To hear that ancient history again was like a dream from which I have just wakened. But above all, I want to thank the Wonder Doctor. He fetched the Golden Speedwell. He went through the greatest dangers. So the last story that shall be told here is the Wonder Doctor's story.'

THE WONDER DOCTOR'S STORY

The Golden Speedwell grows in the far, bleak north at the edge of the snow-line. The exact spot is a secret and may be told to nobody, otherwise I might just as well have sent a crow to pick it for me. Nor could any horse carry me there, for no horse dares cross the Great Barren Heath where every stone conceals a snake. I had therefore to go on foot, and because the king had not many days to live, I walked by day and night.

The first I met was the squirrel, and a little while after that, the rabbit-of-the-dunes. I told them to go immediately to the copper castle to tell their stories. But once I was on the Heath I met no animals at all, except for the wolf who does sometimes venture there. He is fleet of foot and was the first to arrive here, so I'm told.

In the evening I came to the giant oak, the only tree that grows thereabouts. Struck by lightning seven-times-seven-times-seven and yet again, it is full of blackened holes and cracks. There on a branch perched a sparrow-hawk. It was he I sent round to ask all the animals to go to the copper castle with their stories. Luckily, enough of them came.

At the far side of the Great Barren Heath I came across a snake who, with his forked tongue, prophesied that I would slither down the slippery rocks. I didn't believe him, but it happened.

The first high mountains were covered with scrub which served to give me a foothold and to which I could cling. But further up were bare rocks, washed slithery-slip by hundreds of years of rain. Just when I was about to grasp the topmost rock, my numb fingers slipped, and I fell.

Faster and faster, bumping like a rolling stone, I hurtled down, and when I saw the ravine below I thought I must surely break my neck. But on the lower slopes gentle birch trees were growing. They caught me in their springy branches and only my knee was hurt.

Then I saw that snow was beginning to fall, and in my haste I went the wrong way, heading up the valley from which there was no way out. It meant the loss of a whole day, and to get back to the right path I had to wade through a mountain stream. The icy water stung my bare feet like needles until there was no longer any sensation in them and I missed my footing. I sank into the water up to my shoulders and almost drowned, but managed to get to the bank just in time. There I was lucky enough to get a fire going to dry myself, otherwise I would have been frozen into a stiff ice-doll.

The smoke of the fire attracted the attention of a swallow that was flying about. She showed me the shortest way to take, and I asked her to fly to the copper castle at once to tell one of her stories and give the hare news of me.

My path now led through dark pinewoods into which the sun can never penetrate very far, so the fallen needles lie pitch black on the ground. In some places it is as dark as night. Anyone who doesn't know this way will bump his head on the dead branches and his hair will stick to the resin.

I then came to the ring of black lakes. The ground around them is swampy, and anyone who doesn't know his way about there will sink into cold mud up to his neck. White vapours rise from the black water and swirl around you until you can no longer see. But I knew my way and blew the vapours apart until snow began to blind me.

The secret place of the Golden Speedwell was difficult to find, and I had to dig for a long time in the cold snow.

When I found the little leaves, brown spots showed on the green, and I feared they had already been nipped by the frost.

I picked twelve of them, and cupping my hands round them, I blew warm breath inside as I ran back. Once more along the black lakes, once more through the dark pinewoods, once more through the icy stream, and once more across the slippery rocks, though this time I had no free hand to steady myself. That's why I began to look for a way through the mountains, and that's how I found the cave. I crawled inside, struck a light and discovered an ancient chair. Near it, on the floor, lay the skeleton of a witch. A silver ring bound each of her legs, and there was another round her neck. In falling she had upset a sackful of letters of the alphabet. They lay, scattered on the floor in a state of decay. Then I remembered an old story of a dragon, and as I stood musing on this I did not hear someone entering the cave behind me. It was only when he stood there in front of me that I looked up. It was the dwarf.

'What are you doing here?' he asked me sharply.

'What are *you* doing here?' I asked.

'What have you got there, in your hands?' he asked.

'What are those books that *you*'re hugging in your arms?' I asked.

Then the dwarf said: 'Can you read what's written down there on the floor?' and he pointed to the letters. 'Yes, I can,' I answered.

At these words the dwarf dropped the books and stared at me. 'For years I've been trying,' he said roughly. 'For years we dwarfs have been trying to find the entrance to our kingdom. So when I found the letters in this cave, I thought I had found a message or perhaps a prophecy, but I have never been able to read it. I searched in the oldest books that Idur took from the copper castle where they belonged, but I could not find the meaning of those words.' The dwarf gripped my arm. 'Tell me what it says,' he begged.

I answered: 'I'll read it out to you if you'll promise to go at once to the copper castle with those four old books. Take the dwarf's way that nobody else can use. King Mansolain is at the point of death. Maybe this will save his life.'

The dwarf nodded. His 'promise' made me smile. Then I said: 'What is written here is neither a message nor a prophecy. I can read it because I'm a doctor. The letters on the floor form words which tell you how to prepare an ointment to cure broken legs.' And I read out: 'Gli kara, proeteia plaster mastiku, nojpol tsgninto kroskrokko treaja.' That means: 'Take some clay from the bottom of the black lake and smear it on your broken bones.'

For a moment the dwarf stood speechless. Then he burst out laughing so uncontrollably that it took me quite a time to quiet him.

'Well, that's a lot of use, I must say!' he gasped at last. 'But – all right – a dwarf's word is a dwarf's word.' He picked up the books again and went his own way to the copper castle. It was a pity I couldn't give him the Golden Speedwell, but the preparation of it is a secret. All the same, I knew the stories in the old books would keep the king alive a little longer.

I sped on across the mountains; I don't know how many days I journeyed, but I would most certainly have arrived too late had not a special bit of luck come my way.

With a great effort I had climbed the last mountain and found myself once more at the edge of the Great Barren Heath, when there, standing before me, was the only horse that dares to cross it. No snake can bite that horse for he has golden shoes.

'My king has died,' he said, ' and I'm looking for another one.'

Then I said: 'I'll take you to a king who is coming

alive again. Come, gallop faster than the wind!' and I jumped on his back.

Three hours later I was here, knocking at the door, but nobody came to open it. I had to climb in through the kitchen window to prepare this potion and then keep it hot over a flame. Thus you all saw the lighted candle enter the room and now you understand why it meant another thousand years of life, as was written in the dwarf's last book.

CHAPTER FIFTEEN

Hardly had the Wonder Doctor finished his story when a great commotion broke out among the animals.

'The horse with the golden shoes!' they cried. 'Where is he now?'

'In the stables,' the Wonder Doctor replied.

'Let him come in here,' said King Mansolain.

The animals rushed through the copper corridors and soon returned with the horse in their midst. The Wonder Doctor led him by his bridle to the king. 'Sire,' he said, 'from now on this will be your steed.'

The horse bowed his head and the king mounted. In triumph he rode, followed by the Wonder Doctor, the dwarf, and the animals, through the copper hallway to the mother-of-pearl room. There they gathered round him as he addressed them solemnly: 'All you animals and story-tellers assembled here, do you wish to form my new court?'

'Yes, we do, please sire!' they answered.

Then the king produced from under his cloak twelve golden collars and bade the animals to come forward, one by one.

First came the hare. 'You, hare,' the king said, ' you who have served me so faithfully all these years,

you will be First in my court. You will be allowed to sleep on my beard at night, and from now on you will be Lord Hare.' The hare beamed with pride as King Mansolain put the golden collar over his head.

After this, the wolf received a golden collar, and the king said: 'From now on, you will be the Lord Wolf.'

Then he did the same thing for these animals: Lord Squirrel, Lord Rabbit-of-the-dunes, Lady Duck, and Lady Sheep.

Then the beetle chirruped: 'Queekle! I don't need anything really. If I stay cosily in this wool, I shall join in with all the sheep is doing!'

The king smiled and put the next collar over the lion's head. 'From now on you will be Lord Lion. And you...you will be Lord...' But now it was the bumble-bees' turn.

'We cannot serve you,' they hummed, 'but we will stay with the horse,' and they flew round that animal in a circle singing once more their little ditty:

Who has hoofs of gold, of gold,
Hoofs of burnished gold?
Bur-bur-bur-burnished
Hoofs of burnished gold!

'And now, Lord Dragon,' the king went on. But the dragon drew back his heads in alarm. 'No rings round my necks, sire!' he snorted. 'I'll go and live quietly in the copper stables and sneeze fire whenever you need it.'

'Very well,' the king said, and smiled again.

Then the rest of the animals had their turn: Lord Field-Mouse and Lord Town-Mouse, Lady Swallow, Lord Donkey. The donkey looked up with big eyes and whispered: 'Lord Pitiful Donkey really.'

King Mansolain laughed aloud and produced from under his cloak a big hat made of golden-yellow straw with two holes in it. 'Behold, Pitiful Donkey!' he said. 'From now on you will be "Lord Donkey of the Golden Hat",' and he put the hat on the animal's head.

'And now,' the king said, 'now I still have one more golden collar. Whose shall it be?'

Everybody looked round. 'The dwarf's!'

'No,' the little fellow mumbled. 'I don't want to stay here. I must go on searching, like my fellow dwarfs.'

'As you wish,' the king answered. 'Go in peace, dwarf, and greet Idur from me when you see him. But first you must celebrate with us.'

The animals immediately started a round dance, and that led on to the biggest feast ever held in the mother-of-pearl room. Thousands of candles were burning, the choicest delicacies, from walnuts with honey to lavender cake with sea-foam, were handed round. Once more garlands were hung, white roses and pink cherry blossom, and poppies as big as umbrellas were arranged in vases.

The animals did the donkey-dance, the bumble-bees sang a happy tune, the hare played his squeeze-box, the dwarf did a boot-bump dance all by himself, and the two mice told funny stories.

'Aha! Just like the old days!' King Mansolain laughed and clapped his hands from sheer pleasure.

'Be quiet, please be quiet!' the mice shrieked. 'We know a very comical little tale. Please listen for a moment!'

Silence reigned.

'Well?' said the lion.

But instead of a funny story everybody heard a knocking on the front door. 'Open!' someone cried. 'Open the door!'

'Well I never!' the hare exclaimed, and rushed through the hallway. The animals heard the front door open and close again. They heard talking in the hall, then someone appeared in the doorway of the mother-of-pearl room.

It was a rabbit.

He looked startled. 'Oh!' he said. 'Oh dear! I mean...I heard that some stories were needed here and so...'

But suddenly there was a catch in his voice and he shouted: 'Oh dear...MEE!'

'Fliz!' the rabbit-of-the-dunes cried. 'Fliz, I've found you again!' and the two rabbit-brothers embraced until their whiskers became entangled.

'Ah!' said King Mansolain. 'We have no need of a storyteller now, so we will hear his story another time. Instead, I shall give him the twelfth golden collar and he shall be Lord Fliz!'

Then, even more happily than before, the feast went on till far into the night. At last the king said: 'Now we must get some sleep, for tomorrow I shall begin a tour of my kingdom. I shall visit all my animal subjects and maybe even a dwarf, and I shall ride the horse with the golden shoes. Good night!'

'Good night, sire!' the animals cried, and each went to his special place again. The hare on the king's beard, the horse with the golden shoes in front of the bedroom door, the wolf in the guest room, the squirrel among the geraniums in the crystal room, the rabbits-of-the-dunes, Mee and Fliz, together in the room with the statue and the books (the four oldest books were back in their places now), the duck in the yellow iris room, the sheep in the clover room, the beetle among the sheep's curls, the lion in the tower room with the mysterious painting, the ten bumble-bees in the garden room, the three-headed dragon, Breng, in the copper stables, the field-mouse and the town-mouse under the kitchen stove, the swallow in the niche in the attic, the pitiful donkey – I mean, the Donkey of the Golden Hat – in the scullery, and the dwarf...

No, the dwarf didn't go to bed. He was talking to the Wonder Doctor about some burning pains in his back.

'It comes of all this bending down and looking

for an entrance to the under-the-earth kingdom,' the Doctor said.

'Haven't you anything for it?' the dwarf asked. 'Some ointment I could rub on it?'

'No,' the Wonder Doctor answered. 'You must just keep upright and look at the stars.'

'Pooh!' The dwarf was contemptuous. 'I've no wish for anything up there, thanks!' He got up, put the sack on his back, climbed through the window and disappeared among the trees.

The Wonder Doctor stretched himself on the bench near the fire, yawned loudly, and fell asleep as the moon rose and shone on the copper mountains.

All this happened a long time ago. People say that in later times the dwarfs returned, Idur and the Twelve, and with the wishing-flowers they all together uttered a terrible wish: not for 'up there' and the golden city among the stars, but for 'down there' and their under-the-earth kingdom. The copper castle would then have sunk down, mountains and all. People say that Idur found Nemosh there, and that King Mansolain and his animal court have to wait until the snow melts before they can once again ascend the stony stairway out of the fire-mountain.

But nobody knows whether this is true; nobody knows whether King Mansolain is still alive, for nobody knows if the Wonder Doctor had any of the potion left.

Only one thing is certain: under the deep, hard snow in the north, a stone rainbow and a silver tower with a golden sun on top still lie buried: and where once the copper mountains stood, now murmurs the blue, blue sea.

Bree McCready and the Half-Heart Locket
ISBN 978-1-905537-11-2 (paperback, RRP £6.99)

Twelve-year-old Bree McCready has a mission: she has just one night to save the world!

It starts when a clue inscribed on a Half-Heart Locket leads Bree and her best friends Sandy and Honey to an ancient magical book. With it they can freeze time, fly and shrink to the size of ants.

But they soon discover the book has a long history of destruction and death. And it's being sought by the monstrous Thalofedril, who will stop at nothing to get it.

Using its incredible powers, he could turn the world into a wasteland.

Bree, Sandy and Honey go on the run—hurtling off city rooftops, down neck-breaking ravines, and through night-black underground tunnels—to keep the book out of his lethal hands. Little do they know that the greatest danger of all lies ahead, in the heart of his deadly lair…

Can Bree find the courage to face this terrifying evil, and to confront the secrets of her tragic past?

Punchy and exciting, this is a thrilling page-turner from a dazzling new talent.

Jessica Haggerthwaite: Witch Dispatcher
ISBN 978-1-905537-10-5 (paperback, RRP £5.99)

Jessica has the most embarrassing mother in the universe: a professional witch. How can Jessica become a famous scientist when her mother practices magic?

To stop her wrecking Jessica's plans—and breaking up the family—Jessica decides to prove there is no room for superstition in the modern world.

Science and belief must go head to head in this funny and thought-provoking story.

www.stridentpublishing.co.uk